"It appears that you have me at your mercy."

Until that moment, Jane had kept her gaze resolutely fixed on the man's face, but now her eyes shifted to his wound, then skittered away again. She suddenly found herself lacking in confidence and reluctant to do what must be done. The thought of touching that bare, hairy, masculine limb with her own hands was almost more than her mind could cope with.

From her basket she lifted a container of whisky, uncorked it, and was holding it over the wound when a new thought occurred to her. "What is your name, sir?" she asked, her mind shying away from the prospect of an unmarked grave.

"Sebast..." he began just as the container accidentally tipped and a small stream of whisky poured onto the wound. He bolted upright with a roar of anguish, jerked the bottle from her hand and said, "I have a better use for it."

He drank long and deep, then lay back down, clutched the bedclothes, closed his eyes, and said, "I am ready now."

Regency England: 1811-1820

*"It was the best of times,
it was the worst of times...."*

As George III languished in madness, the
pampered and profligate Prince of Wales led the
land in revelry and the elegant Beau Brummel set
the style. Across the Channel, Napoleon continued
to plot against the English until his final exile to
St. Helena. Across the Atlantic, America renewed
hostilities with an old adversary, declaring war on
Britain in 1812. At home, Society glittered, love
matches abounded and poets such as Lord Byron
flourished. It was a time of heroes and villains, a
time of unrelenting charm and gaiety, when entire
fortunes were won or lost on a turn of the dice and
reputation was all. A dazzling period that left its
mark on two continents and whose very name
became a byword for elegance and romance.

Books by Catherine Reynolds

HARLEQUIN REGENCY ROMANCE
47—A THOROUGHLY COMPROMISED BRIDE

THE
HIGHWAYMAN
Catherine Reynolds

Harlequin Books

TORONTO • NEW YORK • LONDON
AMSTERDAM • PARIS • SYDNEY • HAMBURG
STOCKHOLM • ATHENS • TOKYO • MILAN
MADRID • WARSAW • BUDAPEST • AUCKLAND

This book is dedicated, with love, to my children:
Linda, Carl and Stacey, and Karen . . . and in loving
memory to my son, Eric. It is also dedicated to my
sister and brother-in-law, Pat and Gene Viera, and to
my friends, Peg Schelle and Dorothy Droste. All of
them have been my greatest fans, and the best book
promoters any writer could ever wish for.

ISBN 0-373-31209-1

THE HIGHWAYMAN

Copyright © 1993 by Catherine A. Nickens.

CHAPTER ONE

MISS JANE LOCKWOOD and Miss Agatha Wedmore, Jane's former governess and now companion, were returning in the carriage from a trip to the village. There they had made a day of it, calling upon the vicar and his wife, taking a nuncheon at the Crown Inn, and visiting some of the poorer members of the parish.

As they bowled along, they discussed the latest news and gossip imparted to them by Mrs. Micklethorp, the vicar's wife. Or, rather, Miss Wedmore discussed it. Jane listened with only half an ear while allowing her mind to wander to other things.

After all, very little which was new or of interest ever happened in Dunby or the surrounding neighbourhood. Of course, there was the highwayman who had been victimizing the region for the last fortnight, but as he seemed to operate closer to Leeds than to Dunby, Jane saw no reason for concern. And, naturally, there had been the usual animadversions upon the depraved character of Viscount St. Clair, but those were neither new nor news.

She wished that she were driving the curricle instead of being shut up in the carriage on such a splendid day. Ordinarily she would have been, but that morning before they left, it had looked like rain, and rather than arguing with Agatha, she had agreed to take the enclosed carriage.

She strongly suspected, however, that John Coachman had spent the entire day at the local inn, imbibing far too freely. She wondered briefly whether she should tell him to slow down just a trifle, but then decided against it. Inebriated or not, John knew this road as he knew the back of his hand, and they were not likely to meet any other travellers on it. Besides, she quite enjoyed a little reckless speed; she liked to think that it was one of her few vices.

"You are not listening to me, Jane," said Agatha in an accusing voice.

With an apologetic smile, Jane said, "Forgive me, Agatha. I'm afraid I was wool-gathering. What were you saying?"

"I was referring to this scheme of yours to take in Alice Brant while her papa goes gallivanting off to parts unknown."

"Come now, Agatha. You are being unfair. The squire is merely going to the Continent for a few weeks, and since he will be accompanied by several of his cronies, you can scarcely blame him for not wishing to be saddled with Alice. Besides, she must be prepared for her come-out next spring."

"Be that as it may, I do not see why he could not have arranged to leave her with a female relative."

Jane's eyes sparkled with amusement. "Well, as to that, I believe the only one with whom he is on speaking terms is Lady Bassett, his elder sister. Unfortunately, Alice does not care for her aunt, and threw such a tantrum at the possibility of being sent to her that poor Sir Alfred was left positively quaking."

"Now that just proves my point," declared Agatha. "There is no handling the girl! You may mark my words when I say that you are making a sad mistake, for I have yet to meet a more hoydenish female than that one."

"Oh, I believe Alice has outgrown the ways of a hoyden, though I will own that she is a trifle wild."

"Humph," Agatha snorted. "She is wild to a fault, you mean. I very much fear that you will live to regret this."

Jane sighed. Actually, she was quite looking forward to having the girl in her household, since she was certain to liven things up a bit. But rather than admit that to Agatha, who had her own notions of how Jane might liven up her life, she said, "Perhaps I shall, but as I have already agreed to take her under my wing and teach her how to go on in Society, I cannot now cry off. Besides, as you know, the squire was one of Papa's few friends, and has always been unfailingly kind to me. I did not feel that I could refuse him."

When Agatha only scowled and shook her head, Jane added, "In any event, with what he is willing to pay me, I shall be able to make some much needed repairs at Meadowbrook. And you must agree," she continued somewhat ruefully, "that I am rather well suited for teaching proper behaviour to the girl."

Agatha sniffed. She could not argue with that. She would wager that there was not a more proper female in all of England than Miss Jane Lockwood. How often she had wished that it were not so, that Jane were not quite such a pattern card of propriety. Things might have turned out so differently if only... But that was like wishing for the moon.

Well aware of her companion's thoughts, Jane turned her head to glance out the window. They were passing Ethridge Hall and, unconsciously, she leaned forward to get a better view of it. As she did each time she saw it, she wondered why it was that the place fascinated her so, and she felt a surge of sadness that it had been so neglected.

It was built in the Elizabethan style, and its mellow red brick glowed warmly in the afternoon sun. In that light and from this distance, the signs of neglect were not so evident, if one could contrive to ignore the overgrown gardens and parkland surrounding it. And, as always, Jane found herself imagining elegant lords and ladies in old-fashioned dress gliding through the halls and the many rooms of the house. If anyone had ever accused her of having a romantic streak in her nature, she would have denied it vehemently. Yet the thought of all the dramas, loves and intrigues which must have occurred within those walls never failed to stir her.

Ethridge Hall soon passed from sight, however, and Jane sat back, still regretting such waste. The house had sat empty for two years, ever since the death of old Thomas Caldwell, but even before that, the estate had begun to go to ruin. The old man was rumoured to have been as rich as Croesus, but a pinchpenny who had begrudged every farthing he was forced to spend.

Idly, she wondered about Caldwell's heir and why he had never come even to look the place over. Not that she wished for such as he to take up residence there. Viscount St. Clair was said to be the most shocking rake, with a reputation so black that no one would speak of what he had actually done to deserve it. But the least he could have done was sell the estate to someone who would have appreciated it and restored it to its former glory.

A SHORT DISTANCE ahead, the rider of a large black stallion spoke rather apologetically to the horse as he brought him to a halt. "I hate to tell you this, Achilles, but I do not recognize this lane at all. In fact, my friend, I fear we are lost."

The sleek animal tossed his head up and down once, as though he were agreeing with his master, then gave a loud blow through his nostrils which sounded very much like a snort of disgust.

The man had been looking speculatively up and down what he could see of the narrow country lane, but at the noise, he turned his attention to the horse with an amused chuckle. "Yes, I know," he said. "Ridiculous, is it not, to be forced to admit to being lost when I have always prided myself on my sense of direction. But there it is." Then he frowned and muttered, "And it is damnably inconvenient, too."

Horse and rider stood just beside the barrier of a low hedge which bordered the lane. To their left was a small stand of trees, and beyond that the dusty lane curved out of sight. As yet, no one was aware of the stranger's presence in this area of Yorkshire, and he would have preferred to keep it that way. But now he urged his mount towards a small opening he had spied in the hedge, saying, "Well, since there is little danger that anyone in this backwater will recognize me, I think there is nothing for it but to find someone who can point us in the right direction." He stopped and listened for a moment, then added, "And I believe we are in luck."

The distinctive sound of a carriage approaching could be heard, and the rider guided Achilles through the hedge and out into the middle of the lane. There he drew his mount to a halt and waited for the vehicle to appear round the bend.

A few moments later, when a team of horses came into view, he stood in the stirrups and raised an arm to hail the approaching carriage.

As THEY SWEPT around the curve in the lane, Jane broke off her thoughts about Ethridge Hall and grabbed the leather strap in order to keep her balance. It was a good thing she did, for otherwise she would have landed in an undignified heap upon the floor along with Agatha as the carriage was pulled to an abrupt halt. At the same time, she heard John Coachman shout something which sounded very like a warning, and then came the deafening explosion of a gunshot.

Agatha emitted one shrill scream and then began to moan, and Jane took a moment to ascertain that her companion was uninjured. Only when she had satisfied herself on that point did she straighten her bonnet, smooth her gloves, and open the door, preparatory to leaving the carriage. John had not come to help her alight, but she managed to jump to the ground as gracefully as possible. Then she stepped forward to find out what had caused the commotion.

She stopped upon seeing that a man lay motionless in the road. A magnificent black stallion stood beside him, nudging him with its nose.

John Coachman still sat on the box with a smoking pistol in his hand. Upon seeing her, he said, with an odd blend of horror and pride, " 'Tis the highwayman, miss. I've kilt him."

"Nonsense!" said Jane, striding towards the unfortunate victim of her inebriated coachman. "Highwaymen do not hold up carriages in broad daylight!"

Climbing down to follow her, John insisted, "But he was standin' there, blockin' the road, miss, on that great black beast, just like they say the highwayman rides."

At that, Jane knew a moment of doubt, but she quickly brushed it aside, saying, "I should think that a highwayman would be wearing a mask and brandishing a pistol. What is more, I doubt that he would be wearing the costume of a gentleman dressed for riding."

In one swift glance, she had taken in the hapless stranger's appearance and more. He wore buff-

coloured breeches, polished black riding boots and a
claret coat, exquisitely cut and tailored to fit his broad-
shouldered form. In addition, she noted that he was
still breathing, but he was losing a great deal of blood
from a wound rather high up on the inner aspect of his
left lower limb. The fact that he was uncommonly
handsome was of no importance whatever.

At least that was what she told herself, but in all
honesty, she found that she was both attracted and
repelled by him. Attracted because he was, without
doubt, the best-looking man she had ever seen, and
repelled because she could not help but suspect that he
actually was the highwayman. Oddly enough, however, the very thing which repelled her also gave her a
secret thrill. Or perhaps it wasn't so odd, she thought.
Most likely the hint of danger added spice to the situation, which in turn served to make the man more
attractive.

She quickly banished these thoughts, and dropped
to her knees beside him. She untied and removed his
cravat, folded it into a pad, and after the barest of
pauses, gingerly placed it over the wound and applied
pressure. It was extremely embarrassing, not to mention highly improper, to be touching a man so inti-
mately, but she told herself bracingly that the saving
of a life must certainly take precedence over propriety.

Despite that conclusion, she could feel the heat of a
blush on her face, and she kept her head lowered as
she gave instructions to the coachman. Although she
had not needed it today, she always carried her basket

of remedies and medical supplies with her on her trips
to the village. For years she had been fascinated by the
study of herbs and their medicinal uses, and the people of the area depended upon her to treat their ill-
nesses and injuries.

John, much sobered, hurriedly fetched the requested article from the carriage for her.

Selecting a roll of lint from the basket, she secured
the folded cravat to the wound, then sat back on her
heels to decide what best to do.

Dunby could not boast of having a doctor, the
nearest one being in Leeds, but even had there been
one in the village, she would not have considered taking the injured man to him. She quite agreed with the
Duke of Wellington, who was of the opinion that all
doctors were, to a greater or lesser degree, quacks.
Besides, the stranger needed immediate attention, and
the village was much too far away. He might very well
bleed to death before they arrived. Clearly the only
thing to be done was to take him home to Meadowbrook.

By this time, Agatha had joined them. Looking up
at her and John Coachman, Jane said, "Help me to
lift him into the carriage, please. I cannot care for him
here. We must get him to Meadowbrook as quickly as
possible."

"You do not mean to install him there!" exclaimed
Agatha.

"I do," Jane answered. "It is the closest place, and
if we do not stop this bleeding soon, he may yet die.
Now, will you or will you not help me?"

She was well aware of the impropriety of admitting a strange gentleman into her spinster household, and fully expected further objections from her companion.

Surprisingly, however, Agatha, after staring intently at the stranger for a moment, only said, "I daresay you are right. He does look a trifle pale, does he not?"

The unconscious man also proved to be exceedingly tall and well built. But between the three of them, they managed to carry him to the carriage and place him on one of the seats. Of course he did not fit, so it was necessary to lay him on his side with his knees bent, a position which could not have been good for his wound, but it could not be helped.

The two women settled themselves on the opposite seat while John tethered the black stallion to the back of the carriage. Soon they were on their way once more.

After again staring for a few minutes at the man lying across from them, Agatha said, "I wonder who he can be."

"I haven't the least notion," replied Jane. "He could be a guest at one of the houses in the area, but if that is so, it is odd that Mrs. Micklethorp did not mention it."

"Mmm," murmured Agatha. "There is always the possibility that he is, indeed, the highwayman. They do say that he rides a large black horse, and there is nothing to say that a highwayman may not dress as a gentleman."

That thought did not sit well with Jane, but she only said, "Well, in any event, he can do us no harm in his present condition."

Before they could speculate further, they arrived at Meadowbrook and Jane was concerned with the problem of getting her patient transferred from the carriage to a guest bedchamber. Luckily they now had help in the form of Jackson, the groom, and Melrose, the butler, and so the chore went more easily this time. And while the men carried their burden upstairs, Jane collected her basket of medical supplies and went to gather some other items she thought she might need.

It was not until a few minutes later, when she stood outside the chamber where the stranger was being put to bed, that she experienced her first misgivings. Common sense warred with propriety.

While moving the man from the lane to the carriage earlier, she had ascertained that there was no exit wound on the back of his limb. Therefore, the bullet was still in him and must be removed. Although she had never before been called upon to perform such an operation, she did not doubt for a moment that she was the most qualified person to do it.

Of course, a lady should never enter a gentleman's bedchamber, especially when the gentleman in question is a stranger. And to even consider looking upon his bare limb, let alone touching it, was unthinkable. Still, there was no doubt in Jane's mind as to what she must do.

Just then, Jackson and Melrose came out of the chamber and Melrose said, "We have made the gentleman as comfortable as possible, miss. However, I am afraid the wound has begun bleeding again."

Jackson asked, "Was you wishin' me to ride to Leeds for the doctor, miss?"

"No," said Jane distractedly, "there is not time. The bullet is still in the man's, ah, wound and must be removed without delay. I shall need both of you to help me, of course."

Melrose was seldom thrown off stride, but now a look of shock crossed his face. "Miss Jane," he exclaimed, "you cannot be thinking of doing this yourself!"

"Certainly I am," she replied. "There is no one better suited for it than I."

"Now there you are wrong, miss," he contradicted her with all the assurance of an old family retainer. "It will be much more suitable for Jackson to do the job."

Jackson's eyes fairly started from his head, and he backed up a step as he said, "Oh, no! I couldn't!"

"Do not be such a clodpoll," recommended the butler. "You have treated all manner of ailments in horses. There is no reason why you cannot do this."

Appealing to his mistress, Jackson said, "Beggin' your pardon, miss, but a man ain't no horse. Besides, I ain't never dug no bullet outen a horse, never mind no man."

Melrose opened his mouth to argue further, but an exasperated Jane forestalled him by raising a hand and saying, "Enough! We are wasting time."

"But, miss—"

"If you continue to argue, the man will most certainly die, from loss of blood if not from infection. Do you wish to have his death on your conscience?"

Both men looked sheepish but offered no further objections, and Jane said, "Very good. Now, Melrose, please find Miss Wedmore and bring her here immediately. Jackson, you come with me. I very much fear that it may take both of you to restrain our guest if he should regain his senses."

With that, she turned and stepped through the doorway, only to stop abruptly just over the threshold.

Nothing in all her eight and twenty years had ever prepared Miss Jane Lockwood for the sight which now met her eyes. On the bed sprawled the stranger, his head and torso elevated on one elbow and turned towards the door. The sheet had slipped down and now covered only the lower portion of his body, with one hairy limb—the wounded one—exposed. She noted that the other hand gripped the appendage just above the wound before her stunned gaze moved upwards past an equally hairy and quite muscular chest to the face.

Despite the shock of finding herself staring at a nearly naked male, it was the face which came close to undoing Jane. She had never seen anything so threatening in her life. His teeth were bared in a ferocious grimace, his brows lowered in a fierce scowl, and glittering black eyes glared at her menacingly.

Jane's first thought, quickly suppressed, was *Goodness, what a magnificent-looking specimen!* Her second was that she could well believe that this dangerous-looking man might, indeed, be a highwayman. Her third was, *Good heavens, how have I, of all people, ever managed to get myself into such an alarming and indecorous situation?*

No matter what the man's station in life, however, she felt somewhat responsible for his present condition, since it was her coachman—her inebriated coachman—who had caused it. And even a highwayman did not deserve to be left to the inevitable fate which awaited him if his injury remained untreated. Therefore, gathering her courage and assuming a calmness she did not feel, she forced herself to move toward her patient. A patient who looked to be extremely angry and who, she feared, was in no mood to be cooperative.

CHAPTER TWO

GRIPPING HIS THIGH in a vain attempt to control the excruciating pain there, the wounded man thought, *Lord! It hurts like the very devil!* Perspiration popped out on his brow and he fought against the waves of faintness which threatened to overcome him. To make matters worse, his head hurt almost as much, too, and he supposed he must have struck it when he fell from his horse.

Past experience had taught him that the best way to take one's mind off physical discomfort was to concentrate on something else. To that end, he stared at the female who had entered the room on the heels of those two Friday-faced minions who had deprived him of his clothing, then left him to bleed to death.

As a means of distraction, she left much to be desired, and he needed only one glance to take her measure. To begin with, she looked to be far past her prime. She was also something of a Long Meg, being rather taller than the average female. Her hair, partially covered by a lacy white cap, was a soft, though unremarkable shade of brown. And her gown, while obviously of the finest material and well made, was not designed to show off her feminine attributes to any advantage.

If she even had any feminine attributes to show off, he thought sourly. He had no means of knowing whether or not she were married, but everything about her fairly shouted Ape Leader. To do her justice, however, she did possess a rather fine pair of clear, grey eyes.

Had he not been in such pain, and so angry at finding himself here—wherever *here* was—and, worst of all, in such a damnably helpless state, he might almost have laughed at the expression of shock she'd worn upon first entering the room. That had soon given way to her present look of pinched disapproval. It took no imagination whatever to know that this female had never before been presented with the sight of an unclothed male.

He watched her warily as she approached the bed and, in order to retain some control over his situation, he forestalled anything she might say by demanding, "Where the devil am I?"

A small, strained smile had begun to form on her lips, but at his words she pressed them firmly together once more before replying, in a surprisingly civil tone, "You are at Meadowbrook, sir. My home. And I am..."

He did not hear the remainder of her speech, for his senses began to dim as another wave of faintness washed over him. He squeezed his eyes shut as he fought it. When it finally passed, he spoke through gritted teeth. "And how is it that I find myself an unwilling guest here, ma'am?"

A frown of concern creased her brow, but he was far too occupied with more immediate matters to note it.

"I shall be happy to answer your questions, sir," she said. "But at a later time, if you please. For now, suffice it to say that you have been shot; that the bullet is still in the wound; and that it must be removed and the bleeding stopped if you are to survive. I am sorry to state the matter so bluntly, but that is the truth in a nutshell."

"Bloody hell!" he muttered. Then, glancing behind her and seeing only one of the minions, he said, "In that case, I hope you have sent for a doctor."

From the expressions which crossed her face, he was certain that he could see into her mind with a great deal of accuracy. Quite obviously, she was magnanimously suppressing her natural instinct to object to his language. He felt certain, too, that she was attempting to make allowances for a man who was in a great deal of pain as well as weakened from loss of blood. It was a pity that he was not able, just now, to appreciate fully the humour of it all.

She said, injecting a tone of rueful amusement into her voice, "Well, as to that, I am afraid that there is no doctor available."

His eyes had closed again, but now they shot open in another furious glare.

Before he could treat her to more of what she undoubtedly considered his offensive utterances, she rushed into speech again. "However, sir, you are fortunate in that I have some knowledge of the healing arts. In fact, at the risk of sounding conceited, I am considered to be something of an expert in that area, and in the absence of a physician, I propose to remove the bullet myself."

"The hell you will!"

Her mouth compressed once more, but she merely raised her eyebrows and said, "Very well, sir. If not I, then Jackson, my groom, will do it." Then she said with an air of exaggerated innocence, "He has treated all manner of ailments in horses."

At that, he narrowed his eyes at her and gritted his teeth again. Ominously, he said, "I am no horse, madam. I insist that you send for a doctor. If I must have someone digging into me with a knife, I want a real sawbones, not a damned horse-quack."

"My dear sir, the nearest...ah, sawbones...is in Leeds and it would be hours before he could arrive. I fear you must choose between me and Jackson."

At that, his eyes closed again. He dropped back onto the bed, then gasped at the pain caused by the sudden movement and clutched at his leg once more.

What in damnation had he ever done to deserve this? He had the dubious choice of entrusting his life and limb to a ham-handed horse doctor or to this female who considered herself to be an expert in the "healing arts." Likely her expertise consisted of nothing more than waving a vinaigrette or a handful of burnt feathers under the noses of other vapourish females.

But, loath though he was to admit it, he knew her to be right in one respect. Something must be done, and done soon. Already he felt as weak as a sick kitten, and he was holding on to consciousness by a mere thread. And so, there really was no choice at all, was there? At least she didn't look to be ham-handed.

With weary resignation, he growled, "Very well. Get on with it then—you, not that fugitive from a stable. It appears that you have me at your mercy."

Until that moment, Jane had kept her gaze resolutely fixed on the man's face, but now her eyes shifted to his wound, then skittered away again. She suddenly found herself lacking in confidence and more reluctant than ever to do what must be done. She knew that she must, but the thought of touching that bare, hairy, masculine limb with her own hands—without even the benefit of her gloves and his breeches between them—was almost more than her mind could cope with. It would have been difficult enough if he had remained unconscious, but with him awake...

Abruptly she turned away towards the wash-basin, and was grateful to note that Agatha and Melrose had entered the room and were hovering just inside the doorway beside Jackson. Their presence served to bolster her courage and add some much needed stiffness to her backbone.

She required her companion present to lend at least a measure of propriety to the situation, and as she began scrubbing her hands, she said, "I know this will not be pleasant for you, Agatha, but I thank you for coming."

Agatha merely nodded and said, "We are out of laudanum, so I have sent Elsie to procure some. Is there anything more I can do to help?"

"No," Jane replied. "Just the fact of your being here is a great help to me. As for the laudanum, we shall need it later, but I doubt it would take effect soon enough to be of use to us now." Then, turning her attention to the men, she said, "Melrose, I shall need you and Jackson to stand ready to restrain the patient, should it become necessary."

Looking very like men on their way to the gallows, the two crossed the room, Melrose going to the head of the bed and Jackson to the foot.

Jane, after pulling the low bedside table closer and arranging her basket upon it, eyed the two chairs in the chamber. But, judging that either of them would be too low for her purposes, she sat gingerly upon the edge of the bed beside the stranger's exposed knee. From her basket she lifted a container of Scotch whisky, uncorked it, and was holding it over the wound when a new thought suddenly occurred to her. There was a very real chance that this man might yet die, from infection if not from blood loss, and they did not even know his name. Her mind shied away from the thought of an unmarked grave.

Determined, before beginning, to discover that much at least, she asked, "What is your name, sir?"

He was lying perfectly still with his eyes closed, the only sign of tension being his clenched jaw and his hands gripping the linens on either side of him. Relaxing his jaw, he said, "Sebast..."

As he spoke, the container accidentally tipped, and a small stream of whisky poured onto the wound. He bolted upright with a roar of anguish, and his hand shot out to grip her wrist like a vise. His black eyes glaring into hers once more, he shouted, "What the bloody hell are you doing to me, woman?"

"Really, Mr. Sebast," Jane said disapprovingly, "I have tried very hard to take into account both your probable station in life and your condition. But I must tell you that I find your language to be offensive in the extreme.

"As to what I am doing, I am attempting to cleanse your wound with whisky as a preventive to infection."

At that, his eyes shifted to the container, and releasing her wrist, he jerked the bottle from her hand, saying, "I have a better use for it."

Too surprised to react for a moment, Jane watched as he drank, long and deep. But then, before he could finish it off entirely, she reached for it again, fully expecting a struggle for its possession.

However, he gave it up willingly enough, then lay back, closed his eyes, and after resuming his grip on the sheets, said, "I am ready now."

Melrose grasped the man's shoulders and Jackson his ankles, while Jane took up the thin-bladed knife she had cleansed earlier. Holding the blade poised over the wound, she hesitantly placed her other hand on the naked flesh below the wound. But if her patient was ready, she now discovered that she was not. She squeezed her eyes shut, almost overcome by the very alien and disturbing feel of his hair-roughened skin against her palm, as well as by thoughts of the grisly task before her.

There was no telling how long she might have remained like that—seemingly unable to either retreat or go forward—had the man not goaded her by saying, "Confound it, woman! Do you enjoy torturing me with this suspense? Get on with it!"

That effectively ended her procrastination as nothing else could have done. Opening her eyes and gritting her teeth, she lowered the knife and inserted the tip into the wound.

Though not a sound came from his throat, the man's body stiffened and arched, straining against the hands which held him, and then, blessedly, he went limp. Fortunately for both himself and Jane, he had lost consciousness.

By the time she had probed for the bullet, removed it, cleansed the wound, stopped the bleeding, and applied a dressing, she was nearly as pale as her patient. She also found that she was trembling with fatigue brought on by the strain of the ordeal. Even worse, she had the most horrifying feeling that she might burst into tears at any moment—something which would have been entirely out of character for her.

And so she accepted with alacrity Agatha's offer to sit with their patient, and made her way to her bedchamber to recover her poise in privacy.

It was not until after the dinner hour that she returned to the sickroom, where she found Mr. Sebast to be still insensible, as Agatha had reported when she came down to the dining-room. Jane supposed it was just as well. He needed someone with him since he was not yet out of danger, but once he was awake, it would not be proper for her to be alone with him.

However, she hoped he would not remain unconscious for too long. He would soon need sustenance in the form of broth and gruel in order to regain his strength. Then all she need worry about was the dreaded possibility that he might develop a fever, which would indicate that his wound had turned putrid. But a hand placed on his cool brow relieved her of that fear, for the time being at least.

Sitting down in a chair beside the bed, she made herself as comfortable as she could, then gazed at the man lying there. His head was turned toward her on the pillow, and the candle on the bedside table shone full on his face, making it possible for her to study him closely.

His hair was a dark, chestnut brown, and dishevelled as it now was, gave evidence of a natural curl. His brow suggested intelligence; his nose was mainly straight with just a hint of the aquiline; his mouth was well formed; and his chin and jaw seemed to indicate strength. She had noted earlier that his eyes were not actually black, but so dark a brown as to appear to be that colour. Now she noticed that at the outer corners of his closed eyes there were tiny, barely perceptible lines, which made her think that he was no stranger to laughter.

A most attractive man indeed, thought Jane. Yet his was not the classic handsomeness one might associate with a gentleman. Even in repose she could easily imagine it belonging to an ancient warrior, or a pirate or a... highwayman?

Oh, she was being too nonsensical by half. And even if he should be the highwayman, as she had told Agatha, they had little to fear from him in his present condition. She very much doubted that he would end by robbing them, anyway. Surely he would not repay them so shabbily for saving his life. Of course, his life would not have needed saving were it not for them....

Misliking the direction of her thoughts, she sought to turn them into other paths. She mentally listed the many duties awaiting her on the morrow. There were the linens to be sorted, and of course many of them would be in need of mending. They always were. Thank heaven Cook was able to function with only a modicum of supervision. Unfortunately, the same could not be said of Elsie, the young and rather inept maid.

In addition she must meet with Phillips, her estate agent. Their meetings never failed to throw her into a state of gloom. Then, too, she must find time to visit her herb garden and replenish her medicinal supplies, but she considered that a pleasure rather than a chore.

Jane suddenly yawned, shifted to a more comfortable position in her chair, and returned to her ruminations. There was also the necessity of preparing a chamber for young Alice Brant, who would be coming to stay at Meadowbrook in a few days. Jane was looking forward to that event with slightly less pleasure than before. She was beginning to wonder if

Agatha might not be correct in thinking that Jane was biting off more than she could chew.

In small doses, Alice could be extremely likeable, and even amusing at times. But, Jane now admitted to herself, to say that Alice was a spoiled minx was a kindness; the girl was indeed wild to a fault, the product of a doting father who could seldom bring himself to say nay to her. Now the widowed squire had suddenly awakened to the fact that Alice was of marriageable age, and even he was not so blind that he could not see a few glaring deficiencies in her conduct.

"I'll not deny that my young puss is a handful," he had said jovially. "But you will know just how to handle her."

Well, somehow she would manage to bring the girl up to snuff, if only because she must. She deplored the necessity of accepting payment for the task, but, unfortunately, she was in no position to refuse it. Her own papa had left her with a modest competence which was quite sufficient for everyday needs. But there never seemed to be enough money for the repairs required to keep Meadowbrook up as it should be kept.

Jane's heavy-lidded eyes returned to the bed, and a vague thought drifted through her mind. She hoped that her patient would be able to travel soon. There was a certain incongruity in her trying to teach a young girl proper behaviour while a highwayman occupied one of her bedchambers.

The bedside candle had guttered out, and the chamber was moon drenched when Jane startled to wakefulness. For a moment, she could not think how she had come to fall asleep in a chair, nor did she know what had caused her to awaken so abruptly. But then memory returned in a rush as she heard a muttering and rustling sound coming from the bed. She rose swiftly, certain that her greatest fear had come to pass. Her patient was becoming delirious with fever.

Jane reached out a hand to feel his brow, but before she could do so, he gave a great shout and began thrashing about quite violently. Without consideration, she did the only thing she could think of in order to prevent his reopening the wound. She threw herself across his chest in an effort to hold him still.

JANE'S PATIENT came awake rather slowly, but with awareness came the consciousness of three things in rapid succession. He'd been reliving Waterloo in a nightmare, someone had thrust a hot poker through his thigh, and there was an unaccountable heaviness on his chest. For the ending of the nightmare, he could only be thankful, but the latter two circumstances were not to be tolerated.

His left hand and arm seemed to be trapped somehow at his side, but the right one was free and he moved it toward his chest, only to encounter a handful of hair. Further exploration told him that this was attached to a head, and he raised his own head from the pillow to squint down at the apparition lying on his chest. He muttered, "What the devil?"

The moon was full, providing sufficient light for him to identify his assailant. It was the Long Meg, and she had turned her head and was staring back at him, rather as though she were shocked at finding herself in such a position and did not know how she came to be there. Incongruously, and despite the discomfort in his leg, he was amused. He also decided that he had been wrong, after all. With her lying across his chest in that way, he discovered that the lady did, indeed, possess at least two feminine attributes.

Since she neither moved nor spoke, he drawled, "I have known females to throw themselves at gentlemen, but do you know, this is the first time I have experienced that phenomenon quite so literally."

"Your fever!" she gasped. "You were becoming delirious. I was afraid you would do more injury to yourself."

"Kind of you to be so concerned, sweeting, but if I seemed delirious, it was because of a nightmare, not fever."

"Oh!" she breathed.

"Yes," he continued. "And much as I might enjoy this delightful intimacy at another time, I fear that just now my thigh hurts too damned much to do it justice."

Jane came to her senses at the man's words, and with the realization that she still lay sprawled across him in a most unseemly manner, horror and mortification swept through her. Jerking herself up and away from him, she knew that nothing could cause her to remain in his presence a moment longer. No, not even if he were bleeding to death!

With one hand pressed to her mouth and the other to her fluttering stomach, she fled from the room.

It was not until she was already in bed that she recalled his last words and realized that she had failed to offer him laudanum for his pain. She considered returning to him to correct the oversight, but dreaded doing so. Then she thought of waking Agatha and asking her to do it, and had started to rise from the bed before it struck her that that solution would not answer. She could not think how to explain the circumstances to her companion, who would surely wonder how such an oversight had occurred in the first place.

For a brief moment, she even considered sending Elsie, but quickly rejected that notion. The maid's understanding was not of the highest. The poor girl frequently had trouble grasping the gist of even the simplest of instructions, and Jane could easily imagine her dosing their patient with enough laudanum to kill his horse.

In the end, she consoled herself with the thought that if Mr. Sebast's most recent remarks and conduct were any indication, his pain could not be too severe. In any event, she was quite certain that if it became necessary, her patient was perfectly capable of shouting the house down.

CHAPTER THREE

FORTUNATELY FOR the injured man there was not much left of the night. Unfortunately, he lay awake for the remainder of it, unable to sleep because of the unrelenting pain in his thigh. At one point, he did, indeed, consider shouting at the top of his lungs until someone came to his aid, but he discarded that notion in favour of stoic martyrdom.

Instead, he spent much of that time devising ways in which he might take his revenge upon the insensitive female who had appointed herself both his physician and his nurse, only to abandon him to his agony. He knew quite well that he had done his part in driving her away, but anyone with a modicum of sense would know that a man in his condition could not be held accountable for his behaviour.

When at last sunshine bathed the room and he could hear sounds of activity from another part of the house, he fixed his eyes on the door, waiting with fiendish anticipation for her to enter.

After a moment, however, it occurred to him that he would be at a serious disadvantage lying there as he was, with her looking down at him. Laboriously, he placed the pillows against the head of the bed, then

carefully manoeuvred himself to a sitting position
against them, though the effort left him panting and
trembling like a newborn colt. But with the move finally accomplished, he returned his attention to the
door, thinking, *Now let her come*. He was ready for
her.

But it was some time before anyone appeared,
which did nothing to improve his temper. When
someone finally did come, it was not his nemesis, but
another female of even greater vintage. He could not
recall having seen this one before, but as she was
smiling cheerfully and carrying a promising-looking
tray, he decided to hold his spleen until such time as he
should be faced with its proper target.

She introduced herself, and he returned her good-
morning civilly, adding that he hoped hers would
prove to be better than his augured to be.

Agatha cocked her head and studied him solici-
tously before saying, "You poor man. You look as
though you had not slept a wink."

"How observant you are, ma'am," he said. "I don't
mean to complain, but I fear a bullet wound is not
conducive to restful sleep."

He softened this with a smile of such singular charm
that even a female of Miss Wedmore's advanced years
was not immune to it.

For just a moment, she felt a breathless fluttering
within her chaste spinster's breast before recovering
herself enough to say, "Oh, dear. I'm sure Miss
Lockwood will be very sorry to learn that she did not

dose you with sufficient laudanum to relieve your pain."

The man's eyebrows lifted as he replied, "My dear Miss Wedmore, I was not dosed with so much as a single drop of laudanum."

"Not? Now, whatever can Jane have been thinking? It is not at all like her to be so remiss. But however it came about, I shall rectify the mistake immediately. In the meantime, I have brought you some breakfast."

After carefully arranging the tray beside him on the bed, Agatha whisked the covering napkin away, and he looked down into a bowl of thin, grey stuff which could only be gruel. Beside it sat a cup of weak-looking tea. The expectant expression faded from his countenance, and he groaned before muttering, "I might have guessed it. In addition to all else, she means to starve me."

Agatha's lips twitched ever so slightly, but in truth, she could enter into his sentiments exactly. However, when she had said as much to Jane earlier, she'd received a lecture on the proper diet for an invalid. This she now dutifully repeated to their patient.

After staring at her for a moment, he replied, "If I were not so da—so hungry, I'd send this back to that—that *female* with my compliments. As it is, you may tell her from me that for my next meal, I expect something a great deal more substantial. Where is she, anyway?"

"I collect you are referring to Miss Lockwood."

"Yes, if that is the Amazon's name," he growled.

"Well," said Agatha a trifle vaguely, "as to where she is at the moment, I could not say, but I shall certainly tell her that you asked for her when next I see her. However, I fear she is rather busy this morning."

The man gave what could only be termed a smirk, and said, "I've no doubt she is. As busy as she is cowardly."

Agatha thought it best to ignore that remark, and she merely studied him with interest before turning away, saying, "I shall fetch that laudanum for you now."

"Miss Wedmore," he called as she reached the door.

She paused with her hand on the doorknob and looked back at him.

"Achilles," he said rather anxiously. "My horse?"

"Oh," she assured him, "he took no harm in your recent mishap. He is in our stables at this moment, and I promise you we shall take very good care of him."

"My thanks," he said. "He has seen me safely through more than one difficult situation, and I am rather fond of him."

At that, Agatha frowned slightly, wondering if those difficult situations of which he spoke might have something to do with the nefarious activities of a highwayman. But she only nodded before leaving the chamber, saying as she went, "Enjoy your breakfast, Mr. Sebast. I shall return shortly."

Upon hearing himself called Mr. Sebast, he stared at the door in puzzlement, then shrugged and turned his attention to his meagre meal. The misunderstanding was of no consequence and could be cleared up at a later time.

He was so hungry that, although he would not have admitted it under any circumstances, even the gruel tasted good to him. But when he was done and was once more lying down, he discovered himself to be weaker than ever, as well as exhausted beyond belief. He wanted sleep desperately, but the unremitting pain in his leg would not allow it. And so it was with great relief that he welcomed Agatha back into his chamber a few minutes later and swallowed the bitter concoction she offered without a word of protest.

Thanking her, he handed the cup back, then said, "Miss Wedmore, there is another service which you could perform for me if it would not be too much trouble."

"I should be happy to," she replied. "If I am able."

"My man, Kearny, will be wondering what has become of me. He should be racked up at the village inn by now. I should appreciate it if you would send him a message, telling him that I have been wounded but am on the mend and recommending him to remain where he is until he receives further word from me."

"Certainly. You may consider it done," she told him after only a slight hesitation.

"You are very kind," he murmured, his eyelids beginning to droop.

Agatha gazed at the man lying on the bed, wondering if she should speak what was on her mind. Was he the answer to her prayers, as she had begun to hope, or was he something far otherwise?

Every instinct told her that he was a gentleman, but she could so easily be mistaken. He could, in truth, be the highwayman who had the entire district on the fidget. The man, Kearny, of whom he had spoken, might well be an accomplice, although she had heard nothing to indicate the existence of such a person. On the other hand, a man who was fond of his horse and worried about its welfare could not be too wicked, could he?

In the end, she decided that she preferred to place her trust in her female intuition, for it had seldom led her astray.

That being settled, she sat down in the chair beside the bed, and said, "My good man, I could not help but notice earlier that your feelings towards Miss Lockwood seem to be somewhat—that is, they are a trifle . . ."

"Antipathetic?" he supplied, opening his eyes and offering her a lazy grin.

"Well, yes, though perhaps that is too strong a word. However, what I wish to tell you is that I have been with Jane since she was a very young girl, and I believe that I know her better than anyone—most certainly better than she knows herself. And while there is no finer female than she, I would be the first to admit that she is as full as she can hold with proprieties. Not that propriety is a bad thing in a female of gentle birth, but I fear that Jane has a trifling tendency to overdo it, which is likely why you have taken her in dislike.

"In any event," she went on when he made no reply, "I hope you will not judge her too harshly, for you see, there are extenuating circumstances. Not that I mean to bore you with those details, but perhaps if I were to make known to you a few of her better qualities..."

She went on, but by now the laudanum was taking hold, and he heard nothing beyond the drone of her voice until she ended with the words "...and that is what I wished to convey to you, Mr. Sebast."

The repetition of the misnomer pulled him back just enough to make the attempt at correcting her. But he only managed one word, "Not..." before he floated off again on a deliciously pain-free cloud.

AGATHA WAS FAR OFF the mark when she said that she knew Jane better than that lady knew herself. In point of fact, Miss Lockwood was well aware of all her faults, and was agonizing over them at that very moment.

Although a more youthful Jane would have thought it impossible to be too concerned with proper behaviour—and, certainly, she still knew its value—there were times when she admitted, if only to herself, that, possibly, she tended to be a bit too steeped in propriety. On a very few occasions, she had even shared Agatha's wish that she were a bit less so. But after years of ruthlessly training oneself to be a model of decorum, it was difficult, if not impossible, suddenly to turn round and become something else.

For the most part, she accepted herself as she was, the most memorable exception to that being her one, disastrous London Season years before. She had known how it would be, just as she had known that it would take a very unusual man to overlook all her drawbacks and offer for her. She had not really wanted to go to London, but Agatha and Jane's aunt, Lady Chidwell, had insisted.

By the time her embittered and irascible father had consented to give her a Season, she was already older, by at least two years, than most of the other girls making their débuts that year. That, however, had not been the cause of her failure to "take." Nor was it a lack of looks which had been the problem. She was no great beauty, but she had certainly been comely enough to attract the notice of several eligible gentlemen. Although her dowry was not large, she was the heiress to Meadowbrook, too, which counted for something. At least it had then, for at that time the estate was still bringing in a tidy profit.

But after only one dance and some brief conversation with her, all of the more interesting males soon escaped her for the company of more agreeable females.

She knew that she was considered to be too cold, too aloof, too unbending, even too prudish, but as much as she longed to be more like those other girls, she had been wholly unable to relax her rigid code of conduct. Besides, she had not the talent for flirtation or light-hearted chatter with persons of the opposite sex, and would have felt ridiculous attempting it.

And, of course, there was always the old scandal involving her parents, which was, actually, at the very core of the whole matter. It, more than anything else in her life, had formed her present character.

Agatha, always the optimist, had been certain that no one would recall how Lady Lockwood had deserted her husband and daughter to run off with another man. But, although no one had mentioned it in her presence, Jane knew the incident had not been forgotten, and that knowledge had rendered her even more incapable of lowering the barrier she had erected over the years. That barrier had been raised in an attempt to protect herself, to prove herself to be as unlike her mother as possible, and thus win her father's approval, something which, despite all, she had never been able to do.

But if ever she had doubted the wisdom of adhering to such a strict code of propriety, she had only to recall the events of the previous night to erase all uncertainty. Nothing could have shown her more clearly the folly of deviating from her usual mode of behaviour. She should not have remained alone with that man in his chamber. And she could not imagine what had possessed her to throw herself upon him in that abandoned manner without first ascertaining if he indeed had a fever. Everything within her cringed each time she visualized the scene, and each time she did so, it seemed more appalling.

At that moment, Agatha entered the morning-room, and Jane focussed her attention on the sheet she was supposed to be mending.

The older woman took a seat near the younger one and shaking her head, she said, "How I dislike seeing you do servants' work."

Jane looked up in surprise. It had been ages since they had had this argument and she could not think why Agatha should be dredging it up now. She said, "Well, if you can think of a way to teach Elsie to do it, you will have accomplished more than I have ever been able to do. You know that she is hopeless with a needle, and you also know that I do not mind doing it."

Agatha realized it was futile to continue this line of discussion. She was aware that Elsie was next to useless, but with the wages they could afford to pay, there had been no better applicants for the position. That being so, there was nothing to be done, and since the subject was not what was uppermost in Agatha's mind, she dropped it.

Drawing her own work basket closer, she said, "Mr. Sebast seems to be faring well this morning. Of course he is quite weak, but at least he has no fever."

"That is good," murmured Jane without looking up.

"He asked after you," said Agatha casually.

At that, Jane glanced up swiftly, then down again. "Did he?" she asked, carefully matching her tone to her companion's.

"Yes, and for some odd reason, he seemed to be of the opinion that your failure to visit him this morning was due to cowardice. Of course one must make excuses for the poor man. He was in a great deal of pain and said that he'd had no sleep at all last night.''

Jane opened her mouth to speak, then, as though thinking better of it, closed it again. But Agatha, watching closely, saw with satisfaction the crimson colour mounting the younger woman's cheeks. She was now quite certain that Jane was not wholly indifferent to their unexpected guest. She was equally certain that something had occurred between the two of them the previous night. Nothing short of a major distraction would have prevented Jane from seeing to her patient's comfort, and Agatha would have given much to know what it was.

Jane was feeling extremely uncomfortable. She knew that her patient had gone sleepless for only a portion of the night. Still, she felt guilty for having fled his chamber without offering him the relief of laudanum. On top of that was the unwelcome knowledge that it was, indeed, cowardice which had kept her away from him that morning. As much as she disliked admitting to such craven behaviour, she had simply been unable to force herself to face him after what had happened. But it was more than that.

She, too, had lain awake for at least an hour, trying to analyse her feelings towards him, and still she did not understand them. Even without the embarrassment of all that had occurred between them, he awakened feelings and reactions in her which were completely foreign to her, and more than a little frightening.

Each time she had found herself near him, from that first moment when she had knelt beside him in the road, she had felt oddly breathless and on edge, with strange flutterings in her chest and stomach. During the night, she had decided that these sensations were not at all pleasant and had vowed to stay away from him as much as possible until she could be safely rid of him. She had also vowed to stop thinking about him, but she could not seem to do so. Her first thoughts upon awakening that morning had been of him... and most of her thoughts since, if she were to be truthful.

Even worse, she could not seem to stop the sudden visions of his face—or, God help her, his body—which flashed into her mind at odd moments.

However, she knew that she had to face him sooner or later, and since she did not wish to give him further cause to stigmatize her as a coward, she supposed that sooner would be better. She decided that she would take his noon meal of broth to him and that, this time, she would not allow him to discompose her in any way.

It was a decision which proved to be more easily formed than carried out, for she entered his chamber, shortly after the noon hour, with a great deal of trepidation. Despite her good intentions, she was alone again. At the last moment, Agatha had suddenly discovered something of great importance which required her presence elsewhere. And, of course, Elsie could not be found anywhere.

When Jane had remonstrated with her companion, Agatha had said, "Nonsense, my dear. You are merely ministering to a sick and injured man—something which you have done frequently in the past without a loss of reputation. There can be nothing improper in it, and no one could think otherwise. Moreover, the man is so weak he could not hurt a fly."

Jane could not reply to that without revealing far more than was wise. She could not explain, even to herself, why she felt that this man, weak or not, could be dangerous to her.

Now, as she looked at him across the room, her face paled, then turned rosy and heated, and all those uncomfortable sensations were back in full force. He was sitting up in bed, relaxed against a mound of pillows with that blatantly male chest exposed, and he was gazing at her with those hooded, dark eyes.

A slow grin shaped his mouth, and he said in a low, intimate voice, "Ah, at last. My angel of mercy has come to succour me."

CHAPTER FOUR

ALTHOUGH SHE WOULD NOT have credited the possibility, Jane felt herself blushing even more furiously. To counter her reaction, she pressed her lips firmly together and lifted her chin haughtily before advancing toward the bed, saying, "I have brought you some luncheon, Mr. Sebast."

With hunger gnawing at his stomach, he ignored the misnomer again, frowned at the tray, and said, "I hope it is something more sustaining than gruel this time."

Without answering, Jane arranged the tray beside him and stepped back.

After staring at her suspiciously for a moment, he removed the napkin himself and exclaimed, "Damnation! What are you trying to do to me, woman? Why did you not simply allow me to bleed to death yesterday? It would have been kinder by far than this slow starvation. But no doubt kindness is not your object. Doubtless you enjoy torturing your victims."

Jane's chin rose even higher. She said, "I am sorry if you dislike beef broth, sir, but I assure you that for an invalid—"

"Don't bother to repeat that particular fairy tale," he interrupted. "Miss Wedmore entertained me with it this morning, and I did not find it amusing then. In fact, I distinctly remember telling her that I expected more substantial fare in the future."

"I believe, sir, that in this matter I am more qualified than you to—" Jane began coolly.

"Devil take you, madam!" he shouted. "Either bring me some food I can get my teeth into or I shall throw this swill against yonder wall!"

Jane drew herself up stiffly, and for the first time a touch of anger sounded in her voice. "I shall try if I can to ignore your ill temper, Mr. Sebast, since I suppose nothing better can be expected from a man who follows such an occupation as yours. However, I do wish you would at least make an attempt to moderate your language while you are in my home."

If she expected an apology from him, she was doomed to be disappointed. Instead, he asked irritably, "Why do you insist upon calling me Mr. Sebast?"

Jane's eyebrows shot up. "Why, it is your name, is it not? In any event, it is the one you gave me."

"Mmm," he murmured noncommittally. When had he given her a false name he wondered. He must have had a reason, but since he could not recall it at the moment, perhaps it was best to play a waiting game for now. But, as she was watching him with a puzzled frown, he muttered, "I suppose I am unused to being addressed so... formally."

Her expression cleared, and she retorted, "I can well believe *that!*"

Her tone reminded him of an earlier remark—something about his "occupation." "Why, exactly, do you hold me in such low regard?" he demanded.

Smiling thinly, she said, "Come now, Mr. Sebast. Do you deny that you are the highwayman who has been victimizing this region of late?"

He gazed at her blankly for a moment, then, impelled by a sense of deviltry, he leaned back and asked, "Would it do any good for me to deny it? It seems that you have caught me out. I can only wonder how you guessed."

Despite an unexpected feeling of disappointment, she managed to say, "Oh, it was not so difficult. There was your horse, which is very like the one the highwayman is said to ride. And, although you were not brandishing it when you stopped my carriage, you were armed with a pistol."

At that, he frowned again and said, "Ah yes, my pistol. Where is it, by the way?"

She offered him a smile, and he was surprised how it changed and improved her looks. Suddenly he found himself wanting to know more about this unusual female.

Unaware of his reaction, she replied archly, "You don't really believe me such a fool as to tell you that, do you?"

"No, I suppose not," he said. Then, grinning, he changed the subject, saying, "At least I now have an explanation for why I was shot. I had been wondering if you made a habit of greeting all strangers in such an unfriendly manner.''

Her own eyes now gleaming with humour, she said, ''Oh, no. Only those who ride black horses.''

He acknowledged that with a smile, then, with an audible reminder from his stomach, he gestured towards the tray and said, ''Since we have agreed that you are no fool, I am certain that you will see the wisdom of bringing me some genuine food to replace this pap.''

Jane sighed, recognizing the futility of arguing with him. She could well believe that his threat of throwing the tray had not been an idle one. ''Very well,'' she conceded, ''but do not blame me if it does you more harm than good.''

''I shan't,'' he assured her.

When next she entered his chamber, the tray held some generous slices of roasted beef, a chunk of cheese, some fresh baked bread, and a mug of ale.

''This is more like it,'' he said with satisfaction. ''And now I know that you are, indeed, my angel of mercy.''

Blushing again, she said primly, ''I am no such thing, Mr. Sebast. And I only hope that you do not come to regret this.''

''Never!'' he returned. Then he demanded, ''Where are you going?''

Jane had turned to leave, but at that she stopped and said, ''I cannot remain here alone with you, Mr. Sebast. It would not be proper.''

"Devil take propriety," he said, turning his attention back to the tray. "I want you to stay."

This was met with utter silence, and glancing up again he said, "Oh, don't poker up so! I did not mean to offend you, but I see nothing wrong in having you stay here with me. After all, you are in the way of being my physician, are you not?"

"Well, I suppose one might say that," she answered uncertainly.

"Yes, and so there can be nothing improper in giving me your company. Besides, it behooves you to stay in the event that you are right and I suffer a severe setback as a result of eating genuine food."

"In which case you would be justly served," she told him, trying for sternness but failing. The attempt was completely foiled by a slight twitching of her lips and an amused gleam in her eyes.

His eyes held an answering light as he said, "Ah, and only think what satisfaction it would give you to be able to say, 'I told you so.'"

At that, Jane could not hold back a full-fledged smile as she replied, "Now that is a most convincing inducement, sir. Still, I do not think—"

"In addition," he interrupted hastily, "I fail to see what I can possibly do, in my condition, to ruin your reputation. And if that does not convince you, I shall threaten to rise from my bed of pain to follow you if you should leave."

"You would not!"

"Do you wish to put me to the test?"

"You are an unprincipled knave, Mr. Sebast."

"I admit it, Miss Lockwood, but what can you expect from a highwayman?"

Deciding that she would be wise not to call his bluff, Jane gave in as graciously as she could and sat down uneasily on the edge of the bedside chair. She knew that staying with him was wrong. She also knew that it was, above all things, just what she wished to do, but she banished that knowledge to a far corner of her mind.

"Mmm," he murmured with approval as, having gained his objective, he delved wholeheartedly into his meal. "This is well worth the chance of a setback."

Silence then reigned while he consumed several astonishingly large bites of bread, beef and cheese with obvious relish. Fascinated, she watched his hand as he raised the mug to his mouth for a long swallow of ale, unable to prevent herself from focussing on his mouth as his tongue came out to lick his lips.

And suddenly he was grinning at her.

Only then did Jane realize that she had been staring, her own lips parted, while she fantasized about feeling his mouth on hers. *Dear heaven!* she thought. She had never been kissed in her life, not even by her father, and could not think how she had come to be having such thoughts about this dangerous stranger.

She looked away in embarrassment and said the first thing which came into her head. "My goodness, but it is getting warm, is it not?"

His grin widened, since it was actually rather cool for a summer day. He said, "I had not noticed until now, but do you know, I believe you are right. It seems to be getting warmer by the minute."

She could not take exception to what he had said, but felt, somehow, that she should, and this confused her. Resisting an urge to fidget, she cast about for an innocuous topic of conversation but could come up with nothing. What *did* one speak of when conversing with a highwayman? And it did not help that, although he had resumed eating, his eyes remained fixed upon her with a patently amused expression.

Finally, goaded, she said, "I wish you would not stare at me so!"

"Do I make you nervous?" he asked.

"No—yes. I mean—has no one ever told you that it is rude to do so?"

"Frequently," he replied indifferently.

"And I suppose you do not care for that?"

"Not particularly."

She gave a short laugh before saying, "Well, that was a stupid question. Of what use is polite behaviour to a highwayman?"

"None at all, I should think," he agreed.

"I suppose you do not care what the world may think of you, either."

Rather than replying to that, he asked, "Do you care so much for the opinion of others?"

"Yes, of course I do," she answered with a touch of defiance in her voice, although she did not know why she should be feeling defensive.

"Why?" he asked.

Jane frowned, not knowing for a moment how to answer him. Her mother had not cared a fig for the opinion of others, and though *she* might not have suffered for it, Jane and her father certainly had. But she could not tell him that. Finally she said, "Well, I should think that would be obvious. If everyone ignored the rules of Society, there would be nothing but chaos."

"Oh, I grant you, there must be some rules governing Society, but what I had in mind were those rules having to do with propriety. Has it never struck you how ridiculous and unnatural many of them are?"

"I do not find them so," she said primly, but she could not meet his eyes, knowing that it was not strictly the truth.

"Do you not?" he asked softly, taking in her unnaturally stiff posture and the disapproving set of her mouth. "Have you never longed to simply let down your hair and relax, to do something purely for the enjoyment of it?"

Reminded again of her mother's misconduct, Jane felt an anger out of all proportion to the conversation. And it did not help to know that he was right, to be reminded of how frequently she had, indeed, longed to be free.

But a lady did not show her emotions, and she struggled to contain hers before saying coolly, "I think we must agree to disagree on this subject, Mr. Sebast. In any event, I do not care to discuss it with you. I shall only say that Society can be very cruel to those who do not heed its opinions."

He studied her speculatively for a moment, then shrugged and turned his attention back to his meal.

After a few minutes of silence, Jane asked, "Were you a soldier, Mr. Sebast?"

"I was," he acknowledged briefly.

Jane nodded. "I thought as much. And I suppose, like so many of our fighting men, you were unable to find gainful employment upon being sent home. Is that why you became a highwayman?"

"As you say," he answered cautiously, "without gainful employment, a man is left with little choice but to become either a criminal or a beggar."

Leaning forward eagerly, she said, "Yes, and the real crime is that men who have fought so valiantly for our country should be treated so shabbily on their return. But do you not see that if you continue on this course you have chosen, you will eventually be caught and hanged?"

"Why, Miss Lockwood," he teased, "does the thought of my being hanged distress you?"

Distress was scarcely the word for the emotions brought on by that thought, but she only said, "The thought of anyone being hanged distresses me, and this is hardly a matter for levity."

"Forgive me," he said in a chastened voice. "But what would you have me say? The fact of the matter is that I would as lief be a highwayman if my only other choice were begging."

Leaning forward again, she said very earnestly, "Yes, but if I—if someone were to offer you respectable employment . . ."

He knew that he should put a stop to this now, but was oddly reluctant to do so. He was enjoying it too much. She was obviously a do-gooder, and teasing her was almost irresistible. But aside from that, his strength was waning again. Leaning back against the pillows, he closed his eyes and said, "Well, it is certainly something to think about, but not just now, if you please."

"Oh," said Jane, recalling his weakened condition. "Of course, you must rest if you can. Is your wound paining you?"

"Like the very devil," he said, and watched from beneath half-lowered eyelids to see her reaction.

To his surprise, she merely smiled ruefully with a slight shake of her head before asking, "Shall I bring you some laudanum?"

He hesitated, knowing what relief it would bring, but he disliked the accompanying loss of control. During the war, he had seen more than one wounded man become too dependent upon the drug. He said, "I think not. I prefer to do without it if I can."

It was her turn to hesitate. What she was about to offer would necessitate touching his bare limb again, and that she shrank from doing. But she knew she would be obliged to do it soon in any event. His dressing would need to be changed and the wound inspected for signs of infection. At last she said, "I have an ointment I might apply. It is not as effective as laudanum, but it will afford you some relief. Would you prefer to try that?"

He assented, and Jane left, telling him that she would return soon. But as it turned out, it was a full twenty minutes before she kept that promise.

She spent most of that time in searching for Agatha, but to Jane's great annoyance, that lady was nowhere to be found. She did eventually come across Elsie, however, and in the end was obliged to make do with the maid as a chaperon. She also took the time to collect one of her late father's nightshirts.

When she was standing beside her patient's bed once more, she thought at first he had fallen asleep, and she started to turn away with relief. But then his lids lifted and he gazed at her with such pain-filled eyes that she was overcome with compassion as well as guilt for having taken so long.

She said softly, "I am sorry to have kept you waiting, Mr. Sebast, but I have brought the ointment now." He merely nodded, and she continued tentatively, "It will be necessary to...ah...to expose your limb, sir."

As he drew back the sheet, a smile quirked his lips and he said, "I wish you would not refer to it as my limb, Miss Lockwood. I am not a tree."

"Your appendage then," she conceded.

"Good God! *That* brings to mind some freakish creature with tentacles or antennae. Can you not simply call it by its proper name? It is my leg, or, more specifically in this case, my thigh."

"'A rose by any other name...'" she quoted.

"Exactly so!" he said. "So you might just as well call it by its proper name."

"But you must know, sir, that it is not proper for a lady to refer to it thus."

"Yes, and what a great piece of nonsense *that* is!"

Jane did not reply to that. By concentrating solely upon his wound and her task, she soon had removed the bandage, applied her ointment and redressed the wound.

"Well?" he asked. "Shall I live?"

"Oh yes," she answered with a pleased smile. "I think, most definitely, yes. Of course there is still danger of infection, but for now, at least, there is no sign of that."

"Ah," he said, surprised to discover that the pain had already lessened to manageable proportions. "What an unusual female you are, Miss Lockwood. And a talented one, too, I might add."

Flustered by his compliment, Jane tried to cover up her reaction by becoming very businesslike, gathering her supplies and telling him that he must rest now. She knew, however, by the amused look in his eyes that she had failed to mask her blushing agitation. Lowering her own eyes, she encountered that hairy chest again and recalled her other purpose.

Holding the nightshirt out to him, she said, "I thought you would be more comfortable wearing this, sir."

He eyed the garment, ran a hand slowly over his chest, then looked up at her innocently. "Actually, I am more used to sleeping in the—er— But if it will make *you* more comfortable, I shall wear it."

"Thank you!" she said with just a hint of sarcasm.

He grinned, and moving his hand from his chest to his jaw, said, "Tell me, my dear. In addition to keeping a supply of nightshirts on hand for your male guests, do you also provide them with shaving gear?"

"The nightshirt belonged to my late father, Mr. Sebast," she said a trifle stiffly, "and as to the shaving gear, I shall have Melrose bring it to you."

She then did the only thing she could. She made a hasty retreat, taking the gawking Elsie with her.

Jane had dismissed Elsie and proceeded towards her own chamber before she realized that she was smiling. She stopped in the middle of the hallway and touched her lips with her fingertips in wonder.

She had actually enjoyed much of her most recent encounter with Mr. Sebast. Yes, and what was even more amazing, and rather exhilarating, too, was the knowledge that she had not suffered the paralysing awkwardness which usually afflicted her in the presence of strange gentlemen.

Was that because he was a highwayman? But no, she decided in the next instant. Although she could not have said why, she rather thought that he had at least been bred a gentleman, and therefore, perhaps he was not beyond redemption.

She had taken several more steps, but now she stopped again to consider that notion.

Common sense told her that she ought only to be concerned with getting him well to the point where she could be rid of him. Still, that might take several days, and there could be no harm in trying to reform him during that time, could there? In fact, was it not her duty at least to attempt to turn him from the disastrous path he had chosen to follow? One might almost say that it was fated.

CHAPTER FIVE

"WHAT DRIVEL!" exclaimed Jane's patient, interrupting her in the middle of a sentence.

It was the following afternoon. Jane was once more alone with him in his chamber, but by now it had happened so frequently that it no longer seemed such a breach of propriety. Repetition had gradually quieted her conscience, and she told herself that to continue baulking would be to make a mountain out of a molehill. After all, Mr. Sebast was in no condition to harm her, and in any event, he would soon be gone.

At his remark, Jane looked up from the book she had been reading aloud and declared, "Really, Mr. Sebast. I should scarcely stigmatize Shakespeare as drivel!"

"If that is Shakespeare," he asserted, "then I am King George."

A smile curved her lips and she replied, "Then you must certainly own to being our poor, mad king, sir, for this is indeed Shakespeare."

Triumphantly, she held the book up so that he might read the title.

"*The Family Shakespeare*, by Thomas Bowdler," he muttered, then rolled his eyes. "As I said before, it is drivel. Worse than drivel, in fact, and if you had ever read the original version, you would know it."

"Well," she admitted, "I must own that I am finding this to be rather dull reading. Is the original really so very different?"

"As night is to day," he assured her. "When I am on my feet again, I shall obtain a copy for you."

Alarmed at the prospect of how he might obtain such a copy, she said quickly, "That is very kind of you, but it is not at all necessary...."

"No," he agreed, "and I am seldom kind. Nevertheless, I shall do so. I cannot allow you to continue thinking that Shakespeare would write such bland stuff. This idiot, Bowdler, has managed to take all the fire and passion out of it." Seeing her blush at his mention of fire and passion delighted him, but he resisted the urge to tease her and merely added, "Now, what is that other book you have there?"

"Oh," she said, "it is called *Pride and Prejudice*. Have you read it?"

"No. For a good many years, I was out of the country. Except for the classics, I fear that I have fallen far behind in my reading." He did not mention that his time in England had been spent in less admirable pursuits than reading. Instead he said, "I daresay that book cannot be any worse than *The Family Shakespeare*, however."

"Oh, it is a great deal better, I assure you. I like it excessively, and I think you will, too." Then she added, a little uncertainly, "But, perhaps not. It is a romance and was written by a lady. However, she is very witty and clever, and she pokes fun at Society, which *you* will no doubt appreciate."

"Touché," he acknowledged with a grin. "But I promise you, I have nothing against female authors, especially if they are clever and have a sense of humour."

"Then we have something in common," she replied archly, "for *I* have nothing against male authors."

He laughed and told her, "Now, that's landed me a facer!"

Jane smiled, then paused, fingering the book in her lap, before beginning tentatively, "Mr. Sebast..."

He held up his hand and said, "Please, surely such formality is unnecessary between patient and physician. I wish you would call me Jon."

He could no longer endure being called 'Mr. Sebast.' And although he was not fond of the name and never used it, at least Jon was not an alias. He answered to Sebastian when necessary, but that was too close to 'Sebast' for comfort.

She had been curious as to what his given name was, and, forgetting propriety for the moment, she said, half testing, half questioning, "John?"

Good God! he thought. John and Jane. How alarmingly appropriate they sounded together. Making haste to correct her, he said, "No, it is *J-o-n*, with a soft *J*. I fear my mother was of a romantic nature." He paused before adding, "But if you prefer, you might call me Saint, as many of my acquaintances do."

At that, Jane could not suppress a peal of laughter, and she said, "Heavens! What an inappropriate name for a highwayman. I think I should prefer to address you as Jon." Then a frown creased her brow. "But if I were to call you Jon, then you would be free to call me Jane, and that would not be—"

He stopped her again. "I know. I know. It would not be proper. But, my dear Jane, I thought we had already established the fact that I am not in the least proper."

She shook her head at him with a rueful smile. "Do you know how very difficult it is to defeat you in an argument?"

"Then do not attempt it," he recommended. "Besides, we are not having an argument, we are having a discussion." Seeing that she was not entirely convinced, he continued. "If you are worried over what others will think, I have a solution. In private I shall call you Jane, but when others are present, I shall address you as Miss Jane. Will that answer?"

In her mind, she was already thinking of him as Jon, and after a moment of arguing with her better judgement, she said, "Yes, I suppose it might." She spoke firmly enough, but lowered her eyes modestly.

"Excellent!" he said. "And now that we have that settled, what is it that you were about to say to me when I so rudely interrupted you?"

She looked up, and suddenly her mind was blank, but this was not entirely due to his interruption. It had more to do with where her gaze became fixed, as though it had a will of its own.

He was sitting up, leaning back against the headboard, his pillows behind him, and he was wearing one of her father's nightshirts. Regrettably, however, her father had been neither as tall nor as broad of shoulder as her highwayman. As a result, the garment was, of necessity, left unbuttoned from mid-chest to throat. Until now, she had studiously avoided looking at the exposed portion of his chest. Now, she was not only staring at it, but found herself wondering if the hair there would feel soft to her touch or crisp.

"Jane?" he asked quizzically. Recalling herself with a slight start, she raised her eyes to his face and said quickly, if a trifle breathlessly, "Oh, yes, I was curious about those years you spent out of the country. Were you with the army for the whole of that time?"

"Good God, no! I only fought in the war for the last two years of it, until after Waterloo. I spent nearly half of the ten years before that in America."

"America!" she said. Her curiosity ran rampant. She wondered what had happened to make him leave England in the first place, and for so long a time. But when she heard where he had been, one question took precedence over all others. Leaning forward, she asked eagerly, "Did you meet any Indians while you were there?"

He laughed, then teased, "Why, Jane, I would never have taken you for one of those bloodthirsty females, eager to hear tales of barbaric savages."

She waved a hand impatiently, dismissing such a notion. "No, no! It is not their savagery I am interested in." Then, before she could stop herself, she asked, "*Are* they truly as savage as they are said to be?"

This time he laughed even harder before saying, "Despite your lack of interest in the matter, I shall tell you that, indeed, they are." In a more sober voice, he added, "But I can also attest to the fact that they are among the most noble and admirable people who ever walked this earth."

"How strange that they should be both," said Jane with wonder. "But what I started to ask about is their knowledge of herbs and medicine. I have heard that their experience with such things is considerable. Did you meet any of them? You must have done, since you seem to know so much about them."

"I did," he told her. "As a matter of fact, I lived for several months with a band of the Sioux. That is the name given them by the Americans and the French, but they call themselves the Dah-ko-tas."

"Good God!" she exclaimed. "Were you captured?"

"No. Had I been, it is unlikely that I would be here to tell the tale. As it happened, I was in a position to do a service for the chief's son. Little Fox had been wounded by some American cavalry who were chasing him, and I was able to hide him until the danger had passed." He shrugged and added, "The chief was so grateful that he adopted me into the tribe."

"Oh, my," she breathed. "I should love to hear all about your time with them. But first tell me, please, about their healing practices."

"I shall be happy to tell you what little I know, but I fear it is not much. Healing among the Indians is done by medicine men—or in some cases, medicine women—who guard their secrets most jealously. But you must first answer a question for me. How in the world did you become so interested in herbs and healing?"

"Oh, there is no mystery to that. Even as a young girl, before my mother—that is, before I lost my mother, I used to visit our tenants and try to help them when they were ill or in need. I always felt so helpless, though, in the face of illness, until the vicar gave me a book on healing, and it has fascinated me ever since. But now, if you please, do not keep me in suspense any longer."

Pride and Prejudice was forgotten as Jon told Jane all he knew of herbal healing among the Indians. Although it was something of a disappointment to her that he could not give her the English names for many of the herbs used by the natives of America, she did not really mind. What he did tell her was so very interesting that she lost all track of time.

At last, however, her gaze fell upon the mantel clock, and she jumped up, saying, "Oh, good heavens! I shall be late for my meeting with Mr. Phillips, my estate agent. I must go at once."

He grasped her hand before she could turn away, and said, "Come back to me when you are done."

She looked down at her hand, which had never looked so dainty and feminine as it now did, clasped in his own larger, stronger one. She swallowed before saying doubtfully, "I don't know. I have already spent hours with you, and . . ." Her voice trailed off.

"But there is so much more I wish to tell you about my life with the Indians. For instance, there are their courtship and marriage customs, which I know will fascinate you."

Heat rose in her cheeks, but she gave him an indulgent smile as she said accusingly, "I believe you delight in making me blush, sir."

"I do," he admitted, "for it is vastly becoming to you."

"I must go," she said again, attempting to pull her hand free.

He retained it, saying, "I'll not let you leave until I have your promise to return. You cannot know what a dead bore it is to lie here with none but my own company."

"Well," she conceded, "perhaps later, after dinner. But you must promise not to put me to the blush with your stories."

He grinned. "You make it very difficult for me, my dear, but I shall do my best."

Daringly, Jane cocked an eyebrow at him and asked, "Your best to make me blush, or to refrain from doing so?"

"You are too clever by half, sweetheart," he answered.

Jane quickly left the room to the sound of his laughter. But she did not mind that in the least, for her heart was singing. He had called her "sweetheart." Of course it meant nothing. But no one had ever called her that before and, foolish as it might be, she could not help but treasure the sound of it. Nor could she help wondering how it would be if he were ever to say it and mean it.

AFTER JANE HAD GONE, Jon lay back, reviewing the past hours spent with her. He grinned as he recalled some of their conversation and her reactions, especially her blushes, which he indeed delighted in provoking. He wondered if she even realized that, at one point, she had used the phrase, "Good God," which was one of his own habitual exclamations. Yes, she was definitely becoming more relaxed with him. Perhaps achieving the goal he had set himself would prove to be easier than he'd at first believed.

At that, he felt a momentary twinge of guilt, but was able to banish it almost instantly. After all, what he was doing was not simply for his own amusement; it was for her benefit as well. It could not be good for anyone to be so bound up in propriety. And it was not as if he meant to seduce or compromise her. He would not go beyond the line.

Glancing at the clock, he saw that it would be more than an hour until dinner and wondered how to spend the time. Surprisingly, he was not at all tired, which ruled out the possibility of sleep. Then he noticed the book Jane had left lying on the bedside table. He reached for it, but after a brief hesitation, he changed his mind and left it there. He preferred to wait until Jane could read it to him. She had a remarkably pleasant voice, rather low and musical, and he had discovered that he enjoyed listening to her.

He shifted his position and looked at the clock again. Good God! The damned hands had scarcely moved at all. It was truly amazing how quickly the hours with Jane seemed to pass and how slowly they went when he was alone. He even found himself resenting the unknown Mr. Phillips for having taken her away.

At last, however, the dinner hour came and went, and he began to wait impatiently for Jane to return as she had promised. But when darkness had fallen and still she had not come, irritability was added to impatience. She had likely gone out on another of her damned missions of mercy, he decided, and was a little ashamed and surprised to discover that he harboured so possessive an attitude. But, devil take it, *he* should be her first priority now.

He was considering shouting her name until she was forced to make an appearance, when he was distracted by a sound at the window. It was not until the sound was repeated that he realized what it was. Someone was outside, throwing pebbles.

With a swift glance at the closed door, he pushed the sheet aside and gingerly slid his legs over the side of the bed. Then he slowly stood—and immediately sat down again as a wave of faintness threatened to overwhelm him. Damnation! He had not realized that he was still so weak.

Another handful of pebbles hit the window, and he stood even more slowly and carefully, and this time managed to hobble to the aperture. He gave vent to a few more choice curses as he neared it, for some of the missiles had landed inside, on the floor.

Peering down into the darkness, he at first saw nothing, but then a shadow moved away from under the deeper blackness of a tree, and his suspicion was confirmed. He recognized Kearny, his man of all jobs and perhaps his only real friend. Though the former American fur trader would never have admitted to any of the softer emotions, he had proven his devotion to Jon by following him back to England and had even remained with him throughout his army career.

"I got yer message, Saint," said Kearny in what was no doubt meant to be a whisper but might as well have been a shout. "I got to tell you, though, it took me a spell to figger out who the hell Mr. Sebast was."

"Lower your voice," hissed Jon. "And if you got my message, and 'figgered out' it was from me, why did you not remain at the inn as I directed?"

Kearny scratched his nose and lowered his voice a fraction. "Well now, I might have, only it seemed to me that somethin' smelled kinda rotten in Denmark, if you know what I mean. Not *quite* up to snuff, as you Englishers say."

Jon laughed softly, and said, "Well, as it happens, I am glad you are here. I haven't time now to tell you the whole, but suffice it to say that I have been wounded and shall be laid up here for several days."

"That's what I was afraid of," growled Kearny. "Tell me who done it to you and I'll take care of him."

"Unnecessary," Jon quickly assured him. "It was an accident. But there is something you can do for me. I have decided to remain in the neighbourhood for a time—"

"Ha!" interrupted Kearny. "That don't surprise me, bein' as how you been doin' your darnedest to shake off that woman what's been chasin' after you."

It was Lydia Cathcart's relentless pursuit of him which had driven Jon into the wilds of Yorkshire, but, having no wish to discuss the tenacious lady, he ignored Kearny's comment. Instead, he quickly told his henchman what was required of him and had scarcely finished when he heard a sound outside his door. With a quick gesture he sent his man away, then turned just as the door opened and Jane entered the chamber.

She stopped abruptly when she saw him, obviously shocked. Then starting toward him again, she exclaimed, "Oh! You foolish man! What are you doing out of bed? How do you expect your wound to heal at this rate?"

"My wound is healing quite nicely, thanks to your excellent care. And as for being out of bed, I thought a bit of exercise might help me to regain my strength more rapidly." He took several limping steps, then stopped, and with a rather sheepish smile said, "But I find that I am weaker than I thought. I fear I shall need your help in returning to bed."

"Foolish beyond permission," murmured Jane as she reached his side.

Apparently without a thought for propriety, and ignoring the fact that he was clad in nothing but a too-small nightshirt, she placed her left arm around his waist, while he placed his right one around her shoulders.

Though it was true that he was far from his usual strength, he leaned on her a trifle more than was necessary, tightening his arm and bringing her closer against his side.

She felt surprisingly good there, and it struck him quite suddenly that her height suited him very well. In fact, if he were to turn her and hold her in a full embrace, she would fit him perfectly. He would need only to lower his head slightly in order to kiss her.

At that moment, they reached the bed, and Jane looked up at him, her lips slightly parted as if she had been privy to his thoughts. He slowly dragged his gaze from those lips. They stared into each other's eyes for long seconds, until it occurred to him that what he was thinking and feeling was dangerous. In truth, he wanted to do far more than simply kiss her. Old habits died hard, it seemed.

It took every ounce of his will-power to remove his arm from her shoulders and lower himself to the bed, but he did so, feeling quite noble, albeit extremely frustrated. He was aided, however, in this heroic effort by the fact that his wound had begun throbbing viciously again.

Jane tried not to think of what had just occurred between them as she saw to his wound and re-dressed it, and neither of them spoke as she worked.

But when she was done and had made him more comfortable, he said, "I waited for you to return to me after dinner. Why did you not come sooner?"

She thought of her discouraging meeting with Mr. Phillips, and of the equally disheartening time she had later spent poring over the account books. But that was her own problem. Forcing a smile, she said, "Oh, I became so engrossed in going over the accounts that I did not notice the time."

Apparently her smile did not fool him, for he frowned and said, "I have not seen you looking so blue-devilled before. What is wrong?"

"Nothing to concern you," she said with a lightness she did not feel. "It is simply that the numbers will never come out as I wish them to."

Looking relieved, he said, "If that is all that is bothering you, bring the books up to me and I shall tally them for you. In any event, it is no job for a female." He ignored her indignant gasp and, frowning again, added, "Although I do not see why your Mr. Phillips could not do it. Do you not trust him?"

"Why, of course I do. He has managed the estate since before my father's death. And when I said the numbers did not come out as I wish, I did not mean that I am incapable of adding them up correctly. As Mr. Phillips explains it, the problem is simply a sign of the times. The cost of everything has risen out of all proportion to the amount of revenue an estate of this size can bring in."

She had not meant to reveal so much of her financial situation to him, but now that she thought of it, perhaps it was just as well. So far she had done nothing about her resolve to try to reform him. Perhaps it would be a step in that direction if she did allow him to go over the accounts and become familiar with managing an estate. If he showed any aptitude for or interest in it, she might be able to help him find a position in that field.

Looking at her thoughtfully, he said, "Nevertheless, I should like to see those books. It will be killing two birds with one stone. I can, perhaps, help you while relieving my own boredom."

"Very well," she said lightly, "but not tonight, for it is very late. I shall have Melrose bring them to you first thing in the morning."

From his look of astonishment, it was clear that he had expected more resistance from her, and she left the room just barely suppressing the urge to laugh. She was still smiling a short time later as she climbed into bed. She was surprised at how light-hearted she felt. Usually it took her much longer to throw off the dismals brought on by her meetings with the estate manager.

She fell asleep with the thought that, at least in some ways, Jon's company seemed to be good for her.

CHAPTER SIX

Jane was still feeling exceptionally carefree the following morning when she came downstairs. Seeing Melrose in the hall, she stopped to make arrangements to have the account books taken to Jon when next the butler went up to care for their patient's more intimate needs.

Without the least hint of the surprise he must have felt upon hearing such a request, Melrose agreed with his usual aplomb, then followed his mistress into the breakfast room.

But when Jane entered the room, she discovered that Agatha, who was there before her, looked as if a small black rain-cloud were hanging over her head.

Taking her own place at the table, Jane waited until Melrose had served her and left them alone before saying, "Good heavens, Agatha, you look as if you had received some dreadful news. I do hope that is not the case."

Laying her napkin on the table, Agatha replied, "Oh, my dear, I fear it is so. At least—but perhaps I am wrong. Oh dear, it is so difficult to know what to think."

"Why don't you try telling me about it?" said Jane calmly.

"Yes," agreed Agatha. "Perhaps I had better. You see, Mr. Simpson came by this morning to bring a chicken in payment for your treatment of that infected cut on his hand."

Mr. Simpson was one of Jane's tenants. She said automatically, "He needn't have done that." Then her lips quivered slightly as she added, "But I fail to see how that can be such terrible news—unless the poor chicken is very old and stringy?"

"No, no! *That* is not the bad news. It is what he told Cook when he brought the chicken."

"And what is that?" asked Jane.

Agatha sighed, then lowered her voice and declared dramatically, "It is the highwayman. He has struck again, and this time much closer to home, for it was the squire's carriage he held up last night."

"Oh, my," Jane murmured with a frown. "So close to Dunby?"

"Well, no. He still seems to prefer the environs of Leeds. When I said that it had happened closer to home, I meant only that this time the victim was one of our own neighbours. I cannot say what Sir Alfred was doing, returning from Leeds so late at night, but you know what he is."

Agatha did not approve of the squire, who was one of the Prince Regent's rather decadent set.

Jane ignored her companion's comment and said, "How terrible for the squire." But her face had brightened considerably, and she continued, "But, in a way, it is good news."

For a dreadful moment, she had feared that Jon had somehow managed to leave the house last night to ply his trade, but now she realized that such a thing was patently absurd. Even were it not for his wound, which would make riding extremely uncomfortable, if not impossible, he was far too weak to have ridden all the way to Leeds.

Certainly, if the highwayman had struck while Jon was safely ensconced here at Meadowbrook, they could not be one and the same person. Of course, it was very wrong of him to have deceived her so, and she fully intended to have that out with him. Still, it was a great relief to know that he was not, after all, a criminal.

Agatha was looking at her as though she had lost her senses.

"Don't you see, Agatha?" Jane explained eagerly. "This proves that Jo—that Mr. Sebast cannot be the highwayman."

Instead of looking pleased, Agatha merely shook her head sadly and said with great reluctance, "It proves that he could not have robbed the squire last night, but I fear that it does not prove his innocence in the matter."

"What on earth do you mean?" demanded Jane. "Of course it proves his innocence."

"Oh, my dear, I very much fear I have made a dreadful mistake," said the older woman, shaking her head again. "And all because I wished so much to believe—but that is neither here nor there. The fact of the matter is that I knew he had an accomplice.''

''An accomplice! Will you please tell me what you are talking about?'' cried Jane.

Agatha explained about the message Jon had asked her to send to the man Kearny, and as she did so, Jane felt the heaviness of disappointment settle over her. She bit her lip as she recalled that just before entering his chamber last night, she thought she had heard voices. Subsequent events had blotted that from her mind, but now it seemed very significant, especially as she had found him standing at the open window.

Silence fell as Jane sat, frowning thoughtfully, toying with the food on her plate.

Agatha watched her worriedly, but after several minutes, when Jane still had not spoken, she asked, ''What shall we do?''

Jane straightened in her chair and said firmly, ''Why, nothing at all. We shall go on as before.''

She had quickly decided that there was no reason at all for her spirits to be so lowered. Nothing had really changed, except that now it was more important than ever to get on with her goal. In point of fact, she was even more determined to try to turn Jon from his wayward and destructive path.

''But should we not at least tell the squire of our suspicions?'' Agatha enquired doubtfully.

''Certainly not! Suspicion is all we have, and that is not enough to condemn a man. And it is not as if we did not suspect from the beginning that Mr. Sebast was the highwayman." Jane did not add that Jon had, in fact, admitted as much to her.

"Yes," conceded Agatha with a puzzled expression. "But do you know, I had convinced myself that we were wrong and that he was a gentleman. I don't know how my intuition could have led me so far astray. It has never done so before."

Agatha seemed more overset by the thought that her intuition had played her false than she was by the confirmation that Jon was the highwayman, and Jane had to smile. "Well, if it will make you feel any better," she said, "I am in perfect agreement with you. I believe he *is* a gentleman, or at least was bred to be one. Furthermore, I do not believe he is beyond being reformed."

"Indeed it does make me feel better," said Agatha after a moment. "If that is so, perhaps my intuition was not so wrong, after all. Still, our first duty must be to get him well enough to leave here, which does not give you much time to reform him. But you know it would not do to have him here when Alice arrives."

Nor did it leave much time for her own hopes and plans to mature, she thought sadly, but perhaps that was just as well. As much as she longed to see Jane happily married, she could not suppose that a highwayman—even a reformed one, with the manners of a gentleman—would make an appropriate husband. These reflections, however, Agatha kept to herself.

"No," said Jane, "but I do not expect Alice until the end of the week, and in the meantime, I have already begun my campaign to turn our highwayman in another direction."

"How?" asked Agatha curiously.

Jane flushed slightly. "Well, as he expressed an interest in doing so, I am allowing him to look over the account books."

"Good heavens!" said her companion, sounding gleeful and shocked at the same time. "I would never have dreamed that you, of all people, would be so vulgar as to permit a near stranger to become privy to your rather straitened circumstances."

Jane's flush deepened. "You know perfectly well that I would not ordinarily do so, but I believe that, in this case, such a breach of good taste may be justified by the result. Do you not see? If Mr. Sebast shows some aptitude for estate management, perhaps... perhaps the vicar may know of someone who may hire him in that capacity."

At that moment the discussion was brought to an abrupt end as both women became aware of some sort of commotion in the entry hall. They stared at each other in dismay as a young female voice was heard over the rest of the hubbub.

Fearing the worst, Jane rose from the table and left the breakfast room.

In the entry hall, Melrose was staring dumbly at a huge pile of baggage as if he did not understand what it was or how it had got there. He looked up, clearly appalled, as more of the stuff was carried in by two liveried footmen.

In the midst of this mountain of luggage stood an extremely pretty girl with blond curls framing her heart-shaped face, and dressed in a fashionable sprigged muslin gown. She was removing her gloves as she directed the footmen to set the various pieces down wherever they could find room. Then, catching sight of Jane, she lifted her skirts immodestly high, climbed over the pile of bags, bandboxes and trunks, and hurried towards her hostess.

"Oh, Miss Lockwood! The most exciting thing has happened. Papa was actually robbed by the highwayman last night! Can you believe it? Oh, how I wish I had been there."

"Yes, I am sure it would have been most diverting for you," said Jane dryly, hiding her dismay at this turn of events. "But, my dear Alice, I was not expecting you quite so soon."

"Oh, well, Papa knew that you would not mind in the least," Alice replied airily. "And you must know how dreadfully overset he was by his encounter with that devilish rogue. He decided that he must spend a few days in Brighton to calm his nerves before setting out for the Continent."

Not wishing to begin their relationship by criticizing the girl, Jane had said nothing about the unladylike way in which Alice had climbed over her baggage. But she really could not let this pass. "My dear," she said quietly, so that none of the servants would hear, "one should always start out as one means to go on, and that being the case, it is my duty to tell you that you must not use such terms as 'devilish rogue.'"

Alice's lovely blue eyes widened innocently. "But that is what Papa calls the highwayman."

Jane refrained from saying that the squire should not be using such language in his daughter's presence. But since it was not, thank heaven, a part of her job to try to change the father's ways, she only said, "That may very well be. But men are free to say and do a great many things which are not at all proper for a lady."

Alice put her hands on her hips and said indignantly, "Well, it all seems very silly to me, and not at all fair."

Jane had difficulty suppressing a smile as she suddenly thought of how Jon would laugh at that when she told him. Yes, and most likely agree wholeheartedly. But before she could answer, another girl, scarcely older than Alice, entered the house. From her mode of dress, and demeanour, it was not difficult to guess that this was Alice's abigail.

Jane regarded the newcomer with a mixture of relief and chagrin: relief, because she knew that if Elsie were forced to wait upon Alice, she would no doubt leave in a huff before the day was out; chagrin because every additional person in the house made it more difficult to keep Jon's presence a secret.

Doing her best to force that worry from her mind, she spent much of the morning getting Alice settled in, which was no easy chore. The amount of baggage the girl had brought with her made it necessary to prepare a larger chamber than had originally been planned for her use. And with only Elsie to help her, since Agatha was kept occupied in trying to entertain Alice, Jane was obliged to do most of the work.

In addition, she was called out to tend one of her tenants for a stomach complaint which proved to be no more than a touch of dyspepsia, easily relieved. The performance of this small service took up the remainder of the morning.

By noon, Jane was exhausted and longing to escape her seemingly endless tasks to see how Jon fared. With that object in mind, immediately after their nuncheon, she set her reluctant young charge to reading a book entitled *Correct Conduct and Manners for Young Females*. Only then did she feel it safe to look in on her patient.

Slipping through the door of his chamber a few minutes later and closing it quickly behind her, she felt distressingly like a sneak-thief.

But Jon seemed not to notice her furtiveness as he looked up and said, "Where the devil have you been? I wished to discuss these...." He stopped, and a slow smile spread over his face before he broke into laughter. "Good God, woman! What has happened to you? You look as if you had been dragged through the brush backwards."

Jane's hands flew to her hair. Sure enough, her cap was missing, and most of her hair seemed to have come loose from its usual neat arrangement. She spent only a moment in trying to smooth it, however, deciding that as he had already seen her like this, it was too late to do anything about it. Instead, she sank down wearily onto the bedside chair and began to tell him about Alice and her agreement with the squire to take his daughter into her home for a short time, and to coach that rather lively young lady in how to conduct herself in Society.

When she reached the point in her story concerning Alice's unexpected arrival, she discovered that she had been perfectly right. He did laugh, and he agreed with Alice's views on the unfairness of propriety. Amazingly, Jane found herself laughing with him. For he had also listened to her tale with interest and sympathized with her plight when she expressed doubts over the enormity of the task before her. In any event, she felt immensely better after she had unburdened herself.

He reached out to touch her hand when she was done. "Poor honey," he said, and Jane nearly melted at the endearment as well as at his touch.

Despising herself for blushing again, she looked away. "Yes, well, I suppose I have only myself to blame."

"I'll not argue with you there," he teased. "But what have you done with the chit? Locked her in her chamber?"

Jane could not prevent another laugh at that. "Don't think I would not love to," she retorted. "But no. I have her reading a very improving book on deportment."

"Good God! If you have managed to command such docility from her already, I don't see that you should have any problem with her at all."

Looking very sheepish, Jane said, "I fear I neither managed nor commanded her compliance. In fact, I bribed her."

He burst into laughter again. "Oh, Jane. I have not enjoyed anything so much in a very long time. But you must not leave me in suspense. You must tell me how you bribed her."

Reluctantly she admitted, "I told her that if she was *very* good for the next few days, we would have a picnic on Saturday, and perhaps go on a shopping expedition to Leeds on Monday."

An exaggerated look of thoughtfulness appeared on his face, then, after a pause he said quite judiciously, "I believe that you have hit upon the only means of handling the girl. In fact, you have made only one mistake that I can see."

Jane knew that he was teasing her, but she was enjoying the game too much not to play along. "And what, pray tell, is that?"

"Really, my dear," he told her with a broad grin, "you must be a trifle less free with your bribes. You must offer her only one at a time."

"I shall try to remember that in future," she said with a touch of irony. Then, noticing the account books spread out around him on the bed, she added, "I see you have been keeping yourself busy."

A slight frown furrowed his brow. "Yes, but I should like to keep them awhile longer, if I may. Everything seems to be in order, and yet— How long did you say this Phillips has been with you?"

"Well, Father hired him shortly before his death, and that was four years ago."

"Hmm," he said, giving no clue to his thoughts. But after a moment, he commented, "I notice that these books are all of recent date. It would be helpful if I could see some of the records from before Phillips's time. Would that be possible? It would give me a better overall view of things."

His continued interest sounded quite hopeful to her, and she said, "Very well. And perhaps you would like to speak with Phillips, too? He is very knowledgeable about estate management."

"Why, yes," he agreed with an oddly grim smile. "Very likely I shall, but not for a few days yet, I think. I prefer to learn a little more on my own first."

Jane nodded vaguely, for his mention of a few more days had reminded her of her biggest dilemma: how to keep his continued presence here a secret.

Throughout the day, she had been worrying at the problem in the back of her mind. The wisest course would be to spirit him out of the house tonight, after Alice was abed. But where could she send him where he would be safe? And even if she could find an answer to that question, once he was gone it was very probable that she would never see him again.

She tried to ignore the feeling of desolation brought on by that thought and concentrated instead on the fact that her plans to reform him would then come to nought. Of course that was the main reason for her reluctance to see him go. That, and the question of his safety.

She had stood and begun to wander about the room as these considerations ran through her mind. Now she found herself beside the window, gazing down at the floor. So preoccupied was she that it was a moment before she realized what she was seeing. *Pebbles.* There was a scattering of pebbles on the floor.

At first she felt only irritation with Elsie for having failed to clean the chamber today, but then she remembered that the maid had been otherwise occupied. Almost simultaneously, the significance of those pebbles struck her. She understood at once how they came to be there. Obviously someone had thrown them at the window to attract Jon's attention. They were added proof that Jon did, indeed, have an accomplice, one with whom he had been in contact last night.

A glance towards the bed told her that Jon was studying one of the account books again, so she quickly knelt, gathered the pebbles, and shoved them into her pocket as she stood again. Then, not wishing to discuss the question of his guilt in the matter of the highwayman's most recent escapade, she walked to the bed and said, "I must leave you now. I am afraid that even bribery will not keep Alice long at that book."

He looked up at her, and she saw complete understanding in his eyes. "And you are afraid that she will come looking for you and discover that you are harbouring a criminal in your house."

She smiled, hoping he could not see how forced it was. "Well, you must admit that it would create quite a scandal, and you know that I am not nearly so brave about such things as you.''

The look of concern deepened in his eyes, and he said, ''Jane, things are not always as they seem. I fear I have misled you concerning certain facts, but I can explain, I hope, if you will allow me.''

''No, no!'' she insisted. ''There is no need. I understand perfectly, but in any event, there is no time now. I really must go.''

''Very well,'' he conceded, sounding almost relieved. ''But I shall hope to see you later, after that young minx has been put to bed. In the meantime, my dear, try not to worry so. Everything will come out right, I promise you.''

Jane left his chamber wishing with all her heart that she could be as certain of that as he.

CHAPTER SEVEN

OH, WHAT A TANGLED web we weave, thought Jon after Jane had left his chamber. He was not sure if he were glad or sorry that she had prevented his confession. On the whole, he decided, he was relieved. He could not imagine that it would ease her mind to know that she had been harbouring a notorious rake rather than a highwayman. Still, he knew that the inevitable had merely been postponed.

In any event, he had a great deal else with which to occupy his mind just now.

He glanced at the account books, strewn round him on the bed, and his frown deepened. He had guessed, before ever looking at them, that Jane was living in fairly straitened circumstances. For one thing, there was the rather shabby-genteel nature of the furnishings in his chamber. It was clear that no refurbishing had been done in a very long time. Then, too, from the very first, it had been Melrose who had taken on the chore of seeing to Jon's more personal needs, rather than some lesser servant such as a footman.

At first the butler had remained cool and aloof, adroitly fending off all of his charge's efforts to draw information from him. But gradually the man had been won over, and had begun talking more easily with Jon, finally admitting that Miss Lockwood employed no footmen.

In fact, it was Melrose who had given Jon his first clue that all was not as it should be here at Meadowbrook. Although the man was quick to defend his mistress, laying the blame, as she had done, on the present hard times, he had spoken regretfully of how much everything had changed for the worse since the late master's death.

Jon lifted one of the account books, absent-mindedly testing its weight, as if that might give him the answers he sought, then laid it down again.

It was true that, on the surface, all the accounts appeared to be in order. It was also true that times were difficult and Meadowbrook was a small estate. Although it was unlikely that it would generate a vast amount of wealth for its owner, it should certainly be doing better than it was.

If his suspicions were correct, Phillips was cheating Jane and lining his own pockets by skimming off some of the profits from the estate. A clever man bent on thievery would have no difficulty in doctoring the accounts. Nor would it be any great feat to fool a trusting female who was unfamiliar with estate management. But it would take time to prove all this, and it appeared, now, that he would not have that time.

The advent of Alice Brant made it imperative that his charade be ended and that he leave Meadowbrook without further delay. With that young chit here, he knew it would be impossible to keep his presence in this house a secret.

Neither would he be able to continue to keep his arrival in the district quiet, he realized grimly. He could not remain incognito forever, however, and perhaps his fears that Lydia Cathcart would discover his whereabouts and follow him to Yorkshire were groundless. In any event, that was another matter entirely, to be faced if and when it became necessary.

For now, he must decide how best to remove himself from Jane's home. But first he must reveal his true identity to her. His dilemma was, how the devil was he going to accomplish both objectives without losing Jane's friendship and goodwill? And—equally important—do it without damaging her reputation beyond repair?

Until now, he had not worried about that aspect of the situation. Melrose had discreetly let it be known that everyone at Meadowbrook would sooner have their tongues cut out than speak of anything that might hurt Miss Jane's good name. But he could not depend upon such loyalty from Alice or her maid.

Damnation! When he had begun this game of playing highwayman, he had not meant it to go on for so long. But, aside from the entertainment it had afforded him, it had become more and more difficult to extricate himself. It was not without irony that he realized the main reason for this. For the first time in many years, he cared about another person's opinion of him.

His thoughts continued in this vein for some time. After studying the problem from all angles, Jon finally reached an unavoidable conclusion. If he knew anything of the world, neither he nor Jane would be able to conceal this fiasco, no matter what he did. Even if he were to sneak out in the dead of night, which he was unwilling to do, sooner or later someone was bound to discover the truth. And, that being so, perhaps it would be best to handle the matter boldly, relying on Jane's consequence and her reputation as a healer to see them through.

Having decided upon a course of action, Jon lay back to await Melrose's usual midafternoon visit. As he did so, his thoughts returned to Lydia Cathcart.

Were he not so averse to becoming a tenant-for-life, marriage to her would ensure his acceptance by even the highest sticklers of the ton. But he could not conceive of spending a lifetime with Lydia. If he were ever to wed at all, he would prefer someone like Jane. For one thing, she was a great deal more amusing and interesting than Lydia. Moreover, she was a kind and caring woman. And, while Lydia was a diamond of the first water, Jane—well, he suddenly realized he found her looks infinitely more appealing than Lydia's perfection.

However, he told himself with a sudden frown, all this was wasted conjecture since he had no intention of marrying anyone.

Melrose arrived just then and listened to Jon's requests without turning a hair. He even entered into the spirit of the thing by making one or two modest suggestions of his own. When next he entered the room, shortly before the dinner hour, he carried one of his late master's canes and a fresh roll of lint, in addition to the requested articles of clothing. His only show of surprise came when he heard the message he was to deliver to his mistress. His eyes widened slightly upon being given the name he was to use when relaying that message.

JANE, AGATHA AND ALICE were gathered in the drawing-room, where Jane had been trying to teach Alice the art of pre-dinner conversation. But she had found it rather heavy going, since the girl could not seem to grasp the fact that it was impolite to push herself forward and dominate every discussion. When Melrose entered the room, Jane rose from her chair with alacrity, expecting him to announce that dinner was ready to be served.

But what he said, without so much as a blink, was "Miss Jane, Lord St. Clair has asked me to inform you that he will be joining you for dinner tonight."

To say that Jane was shocked would have been the grossest understatement. She was struck speechless and her mind was thrown into confusion. All she could think was *St. Clair?* What in heaven's name was Jon up to now?

Fortunately Agatha stepped into the breach after scarcely a moment of stunned silence. She said, "Oh, St. Clair! But do you think that is wise, Jane?"

"What?" said Jane blankly.

Agatha frowned, and with a tiny movement of her head, indicated Alice, who was listening with avid interest. She said brightly, "Well, you know how ill the poor man has been. I was just wondering if it would be wise for him to make such an effort when he is not yet fully recovered."

Before Jane could answer, Alice cried, "St. Clair? Viscount St. Clair?"

Ignoring her, Jane turned to the butler, saying, "Please inform his lordship that I should not dream of having him go to such trouble when he is still so unwell."

"I fear, miss," said Melrose with only a hint of regret, "that Lord St. Clair was quite insistent."

"Oh," crowed Alice, with unbecoming glee, "I cannot wait to tell my friend Clarissa! She will be positively green with envy when she hears that I have actually met him."

While Jane fought to hide her dismay, Agatha again came to her rescue. She turned to Alice and said sharply, "Sit down, child, and try, if you can, to behave like a lady, or you shall be sent to your room and never meet him." Then, turning back to the butler, she said, "Please tell Lord St. Clair that we shall, of course, welcome his company."

As Melrose bowed and left the room, Alice said a trifle sullenly, "Well, I was only curious, and I don't see how you can blame me for that! I have been hearing about St. Clair forever, but no one has ever heard that you are on such friendly terms with him."

Not even herself, Jane thought ruefully. By now, however, she had collected herself, and she replied, with what she trusted was just the right touch of amusement in her voice, "I am afraid that it is not the sort of connection one feels inclined to broadcast. And in truth, I am not all that well acquainted with him. His presence here came about as the result of an unfortunate accident."

"Indeed," agreed Agatha cheerfully. "Nor can you be blamed for taking him in when he was so dreadfully injured. Besides, I do not believe above half the stories which are told of him. And we have found him to be a perfect gentleman, have we not, Jane?"

Despite a strong urge to strangle her companion, Jane managed to smile thinly and nod her agreement, but her thoughts were not at all agreeable. She was thinking that between Jon and Agatha she was becoming more and more embroiled in this ridiculous deception. And there did not seem to be a thing she could do about it.

Devil take the two of them, she suddenly thought. She was a little shocked at how easily the words had popped into her head. Before meeting Jon, she would never have dreamed of using such an expression—at least, not often. Still, she had to admit that it was a much more satisfying way of expressing one's true feelings than any of the pallid exclamations considered suitable for females.

But for the life of her, she could not think what Jon was about. Only for the briefest moment did she entertain the notion that he might, indeed, be St. Clair.

The idea was too absurd. No, this was merely a smoke screen which Jon had raised to hide the fact that she had been harbouring a highwayman. It warmed her heart to think that he should be trying to shield her, but of all the names he might have chosen, *that* one was the worst. .

She knew that Alice was positively burning with curiosity, and dreaded having to devise answers to any more of the girl's questions. She was given a temporary reprieve, however, for just then Jon entered the drawing-room, escorted by Melrose. And all the consternation she had been feeling was swept aside... at least for the moment.

He was using one of her father's canes and was attired in the clothing he had been wearing when he was shot. His garments had, of course, been cleaned, pressed, and patched, and he looked incredibly handsome.

For a moment, that part of her which was interested in all things of a medical nature wondered how he had managed to get into those tight breeches. She decided that he must have re-dressed his wound with a less bulky bandage, before she banished such inappropriate speculation.

While he apologized for his unsuitable attire—for he was, after all, wearing riding clothes—Jane simply stared at him. She suddenly knew that she would willingly tell any number of lies, enter into any number of deceptions, in order to protect him. And, along with that knowledge came another, even more stunning revelation. Dear God, she was falling in love with this impossible man . . . her highwayman, who was just as forbidden to her as the real St. Clair could ever be.

Despite her willing, if rather imprudent, resolve to sanction whatever fabrication he might be weaving, Jane took little part in the dinner-table conversation. For one thing, she was still somewhat dazed from the realization of her feelings for Jon. But, aside from that, she thought it safer to say as little as possible. She could scarcely wait, however, to be alone with him, to discover just what demon had caused him to appropriate St. Clair's identity.

Although she was on edge the whole of the time, expecting disaster to strike at any minute, everything actually went much better than she had feared. Of course Alice began by displaying a vulgar curiosity, bombarding Jon with all manner of questions. But, for once, Jane felt no urge to restrain the girl, for she was as anxious to hear the answers as Alice.

During the course of the next two hours, they learned that "St. Clair" had come into Yorkshire to look over his inheritance and had become incapacitated due to an injury. Since he had found Ethridge Hall to be uninhabitable, he had been kindly taken in and cared for by Miss Jane and her lovely companion, Miss Wedmore.

At the end of his explanation, he gazed at Jane innocently and said, "Actually, Miss Jane, I have been studying the matter and I believe we may be distantly related through my mother. So perhaps I should call you cousin."

Jane nearly choked before uttering a denial. "I think that very unlikely," she managed in a rather strangled voice.

"No, no. I am almost certain I recall Mama mentioning some Lockwoods in her family tree."

Naturally, Agatha threw herself enthusiastically into this new piece of fiction and engaged in a detailed discussion of genealogy with St. Clair.

In spite of herself, Jane was moved to a grudging admiration for the man's inventiveness. But in truth, except for the identity he had chosen and his outrageous claim to kinship, his story was factual and could not have sounded more innocent or respectable.

He also entertained them with accounts of his more amusing experiences in America, thereby diverting Alice and preventing her from asking too many impertinent questions.

By the end of the meal, however, Jane's mood had changed again. She was feeling unreasonably irritable and oddly resentful, for he seemed to know just how to handle the girl, treating her by turns with amused tolerance and flattering admiration, bordering on the flirtatious. It was becoming increasingly apparent that Alice was not only thoroughly intrigued by him, but was well on the way to forming a *tendre* for him.

Great heavens! thought Jane. The man could charm a stone if he set his mind to it. In truth, she feared that her highwayman was every bit as rakish as the notorious character he was pretending to be.

It was almost with relief that she watched him take his leave of them immediately after dinner, using the excuse of his recent injury for his early retirement. Despite her confused feelings, including a very natural exasperation with him, she had, as always, enjoyed his company. But she did not think she could bear watching Alice become more and more enamoured of him throughout an entire evening. It would not be at all wise to allow such an infatuation to develop. That was another subject about which she must speak with him.

As he climbed the stairs, however, she saw that he was leaning more heavily upon the cane than he had been earlier. She realized what an ordeal the past two hours must have been for him. It had been little more than three days since he had been shot, and she knew that he must still be dreadfully weak. And, she thought with a worried frown, his wound must still be giving him a great deal of discomfort, if not outright pain. But even in the midst of her concern, she was aware of a warm glow at the thought that he had put forth such effort on her behalf.

And then, as he disappeared up the stairs, another realization struck her. *Three days... only three days since he had been wounded, only three days since she had first set eyes on him.* How was it possible to lose one's heart to a man—especially one so unsuitable— in such a short time?

Somehow she got through the seemingly endless evening. But, thrown off kilter by so many unaccustomed emotions, she could not afterwards have said how the time passed. Pass it did, however, and when at last she made her way to Jon's chamber, she had reached several unpalatable but necessary conclusions.

As distasteful as it was to admit it, she was behaving no better than Alice where Jon was concerned. Worse, in fact, for one might expect an inexperienced girl to be vulnerable to the charms of a worldly and attractive male. But Jane should have had more sense than to fall victim to infatuation; for, of course, that was all it was.

Thank heaven she had realized that and come to her senses in time. She shuddered to think what a figure of fun she might have made of herself otherwise.

She was not so naive as to think that simply by recognizing the true nature of her feelings, she could instantly overcome them. But infatuation was more curable than love, and now that she knew what ailed her, she would be on her guard. She did not expect that it would be easy to resist him, but she knew that she must, and she would.

It was with this firm resolution in mind that she entered his chamber.

He was sitting up, propped against the pillows, and he watched her warily as she crossed the room.

Her hands clasped together in front of her to hide their sudden trembling, she said, with an attempt at humour, "Well, I scarcely know what to call you now—Jon, Mr. Sebast, or St. Clair."

"Jon will do nicely," he answered cautiously. "Or St. Clair, if you prefer."

She shook her head slightly, saying, "Before we broach the subject of names, I should like to say that

I do appreciate what you did this evening. I know how difficult it must have been, and that you did it for my sake."

She was thankful that her voice sounded quite calm and normal. The wary expression disappeared from his face, replaced by one of his heart-stopping smiles.

He shrugged slightly and said modestly, "It was nothing."

"Yes, but what I should like to know," she demanded, no longer sounding quite so calm, "is why, of all things, you chose to use St Clair's name!"

With one hand pressed to her brow, she had turned away from him, and so did not see his look of astonishment.

Without waiting for him to speak, she continued. "Oh, I am persuaded that it is merely a most unfortunate coincidence. Having been out of the country so much of the time, you cannot know the connotation attached to that name. But, Jon," she said earnestly, turning towards him, "truly, you could not have hit upon a worse identity to assume."

In her agitation she sat down on the edge of the bed and took his hand.

His fingers—long, blunt-tipped, and utterly masculine—closed round hers as a troubled frown creased his brow.

Seeing it, she had an almost irresistible urge to reach out with her free hand to smooth it away. Then, just as suddenly, she became aware of what she was doing, and she moved to pull her hand from his and stand. She was prevented from doing so when his hand tightened round hers, holding her where she was, and, after a moment, she gave up the struggle.

He rubbed his thumb back and forth along one of her fingers as he said softly, "Jane, I hardly know what to say. I thought you understood."

"Oh, I do!" she assured him.

He gave a small huff of laughter and shook his head ruefully. "No, you do not," he told her. Then he paused before adding, "Jane, I *am* St Clair."

She stared at him and the colour slowly drained from her face. "But...but...you are the highwayman."

"No."

As complete understanding finally came to her, she stiffened, and before he could again prevent it, she jerked her hand free, stood, and backed away from the bed. All she could think was that, for the whole of this time, he had been playing her for a fool.

She was mortified, but more than that, she was angry. She said coldly, "Then you lied to me from the very beginning."

"Not exactly," he defended himself. "You assumed I was the highwayman, and I simply failed to correct you. I know it was wrong of me, but—"

"You told me your name was Sebast," she accused.

"I was attempting to tell you that my name is Sebastian St. Clair when that damned whisky spilled."

"Then Jon is no more your real name than Sebast is."

He sighed. "My full name is Jon Edward Sebastian Manning, Viscount St. Clair. While I seldom use it, Jon *is* one of my names."

She stared at him a moment longer before saying in an uncompromising tone, "I see little difference between omitting the truth and lying."

With that, she whirled round and left his chamber, ignoring the plea in his voice as he called after her.

CHAPTER EIGHT

DURING THE LONG hours before Jane fell asleep that night, she admitted some truths and reached some decisions regarding herself and Jon.

To begin with, she was forced to concede that her anger might be due more to the manner in which the truth had come out than to his deception. Her feelings were a trifle hurt that he had not told her in private first.... Well, in point of fact, they were a great deal hurt, but she could deal with that.

Moreover, in all fairness, she had to admit that much of the tangle had resulted from her own assumptions rather than from any outright lie on his part. Of course, he should not have allowed her to continue in her misconceptions. That was certainly wrong of him, but she thought she knew him well enough by now to understand why he had done it.

He had been in pain, and bored, which was only natural, and she had presented him with the perfect opportunity to amuse and divert himself. In addition, he was something of a tease, but how could she fault him for that when she had so frequently derived as much enjoyment from his teasing as he? Then, too, he might have seen this farrago as a rather harmless means of taking revenge against those who had caused his misfortune. One could scarcely blame him for that, if it were so.

All of which brought her to the question of what would have happened had she known from the start that he was St. Clair. Would she still have taken him into her home and cared for him herself?

She thought not. Most likely she would have taken him to Dunby, despite the distance and the increased risk to himself. She doubted that she would have been so bold had she known who he was. But that was a very odd thing: why should she have been more willing to bring a suspected highwayman into her home than St. Clair? It took her several moments to puzzle that out, but finally she decided that, although strongly attracted to him from the beginning, she had thought her heart safe from such a man.

But she had heard too many tales of St. Clair's legendary way with females not to have known the danger of taking him in. Yet she could not really be sorry that she had. She was forced to concede that before he had come into her life, it had been a great deal more dull than she had ever realized.

She sighed as she acknowledged another truth—the most important one of all. As much as she disliked owning to it, she knew that what she felt for Jon was not just infatuation. She loved him, but he did not love her.

How could he? His looks were such that he could attract any female he might wish for, while hers were quite ordinary at best. He was in his prime, while she was far past hers. He was worldly and sophisticated, while she had spent nearly the whole of her life here in Yorkshire. He was a rake, while she was a pattern card of propriety.

No. They were completely unsuited. But, thinking over the past few days, she did believe that, though she could never hope for his love, he had, at least, developed some liking for her, and he might think of her as a friend. That was a pale substitute for love, but if it was all she could have, it would have to satisfy her. And for the sake of retaining his friendship, she would not send him away, even though she knew she ought to do so.

There would certainly be some gossip, but the facts of the case, coupled with her own consequence, should be enough to protect her reputation. In any event, it was too late to worry about that now. There would be talk whether he remained here or not, so he might as well remain.

Nevertheless, in order to guard her heart from further damage, she determined to keep more distance between them. But in this last deliberation she had reckoned without Jon, and without her own foolish heart.

JANE, AGATHA and Alice were already at the table the following morning when he entered the breakfast room. He made his way to a vacant chair and greeted Agatha and Alice cheerfully. Then, passing behind Jane's chair, and before she could guess what he intended, he leaned around her and kissed her cheek, murmuring, "Good morning, sweet cousin."

While Jane blushed furiously, he continued on his way as though nothing out of the ordinary had occurred.

Alice, who had been told only moments before that she must spend the day learning proper deportment, had been toying with her food apathetically, her face a study in resentment. But at St. Clair's appearance, she brightened considerably.

"Good morning, St. Clair," she sang out.

Jane frowned and said, more sharply than she intended, "The proper form of address, Alice, is Lord St. Clair."

Resentment, now coupled with rebellion, returned to the girl's face. "That's silly! No one uses a man's full title. And I have never heard him referred to as anything but St. Clair."

Gentling her voice, Jane replied, "Nevertheless, there are times when it is appropriate to use the full title. In any case, you are very young, and as your elder, his lordship deserves to be shown the proper respect."

Angrily, Alice threw down her napkin and leapt to her feet. "Oh! Proper! Proper! Proper! I am sick of hearing that word! I wish Papa had never sent me here. I thought staying with you would be more fun than staying with my Aunt Bassett, but it isn't! You are just like her old-maid daughter, my cousin Josephine, who is nothing but a dried-up old stick!"

Horrified, Jane watched the girl run from the room. She dropped her face into her hands and muttered, "You were right, Agatha. I should never have agreed to do this."

"Perhaps it is time to offer her another bribe," interposed St. Clair in an obvious attempt to lighten the atmosphere.

He received a rather weak smile from Jane for his effort.

"Fiddle!" said Agatha stoutly. "The chit is a spoiled brat, and what we have just witnessed is nothing more than a temper tantrum. She will get over it."

"Yes, but it is obvious that I have no notion of how to go on with her. Perhaps I should send a message to Brighton, telling the squire that he must make other arrangements for Alice."

"If I know anything of Sir Alfred," said St. Clair, "it is too late for that. He will simply ignore the message and go on his merry way."

"Humph," said Agatha. "No truer words were ever spoken. The man does not know the meaning of responsibility."

"You are probably right," said Jane, gazing down at her plate.

Frowning, St. Clair said bracingly, "My dear Jane, I thought you were made of sterner stuff. You may have begun on the wrong foot with the girl, but it is not too late to start anew. If I may offer a suggestion... but perhaps I am meddling where I am not wanted."

"Oh, no," Jane murmured somewhat distractedly. "I should be grateful for any advice."

"Well then, I doubt that anyone could succeed in turning Alice into a proper young miss, and to my way of thinking, no one should try. There is nothing so boring as an insipid—but that is another matter.

"In any event, since all you can hope for is to teach her the basics of good breeding, perhaps you should concentrate only on those things which are of greatest importance. I also think you might do better to teach her by example than by criticism."

"Yes, that makes sense," said Jane quietly, her eyes downcast. "Thank you."

St. Clair sent a swift, worried glance in Agatha's direction, but she merely shrugged. Turning back to Jane, he said in a teasing voice, "And do not forget the bribes."

In truth, Jane had barely been following the conversation, for Alice's words kept repeating themselves over and over again in her mind. Now, however, she suddenly realized how self-pitying she must have sounded. Forcing a smile, she retorted, "Oh, no. What a dreadful mistake *that* would be. I am persuaded, in fact, that it is the best advice of all."

"That is much better," said St. Clair. "I knew you had pluck. But, my dear girl, was it really necessary to make me sound quite so decrepit? I realize the chit is very young, but she *is* of marriageable age, and I am only three-and-thirty."

Jane threw him a startled glance and said, "No, you are not quite in your dotage." Then, standing abruptly, she added, "But enough of this nonsense. You may be a gentleman of leisure, but I have a great deal of work awaiting me."

The other two arose from the table, and Agatha said, "I shall go check on Elsie or she will waste the morning day-dreaming while dusting one piece of furniture." With that, she hurried from the room.

As Jane and St. Clair moved towards the door, she said, "I hope you don't mean to overtax yourself, Jon. You are not yet fully recovered, you know."

"Don't worry." He smiled. "I know my limits and shall rest when I feel the need. You have done a remarkable job of healing me and, oddly enough, the exertion of moving about more seems to have a good effect. I am feeling much stronger today. And as I am not in the least tired at present, I think this might be a good time to look over those other account books."

Jane stopped, flustered. "Oh, but that was only—I mean, there is no longer a need, now that..."

They stood, facing each other, and as her voice trailed off, he said, "Ah, I see. You mean that you would allow a highwayman access to your financial records, but not the notorious St. Clair."

Blushing, she replied, "Don't be absurd. I did not mean that at all."

His brows rose questioningly, and she said, "Oh, for heaven's sake! Feel free to look to your heart's content. Come. I shall show you to the estate room...unless you would prefer that I have them brought to your chamber?"

"No, the estate room will be fine."

He followed her to a small room at the back of the house, where she again reminded him not to overtax his strength. But when she turned to leave, he stopped her.

Taking both her hands in his, he said, "I have been thinking...."

"Yes?" She hoped her voice did not sound as breathless as she feared. She did not know what she had hoped to hear, but his words surprised her.

He said, "We have become accustomed to address-ing one another by our first names, which is fine when we are in private. But perhaps it would be better if we were a trifle more cautious in future...particularly before Alice. Also, you must be very discreet when visiting my chamber."

A small spark of anger came to life. Was *he,* of all people, lecturing *her* on the subject of propriety?

"Of course," she said rather stiffly, withdrawing her hands. She could not resist adding tartly, "And per-haps you should refrain from greeting me with a kiss on the cheek in future."

He grinned and said, "Oh, well, that was merely a cousinly gesture."

"Nevertheless, I advise you to take care, St. Clair. You know as well as I that no one is likely to believe that far-fetched tale."

With that, she left him and did not hear the small sound he made, which was halfway between a muf-fled laugh and a sigh.

Although she had duties to perform, Jane went straight to her room, upheld by a strong feeling of indignation until despondency overtook her again.

The scene at the breakfast table replayed in her mind, and she recalled Alice's parting words. In all her efforts to be the opposite of her mother, she had never considered that anyone would ever view her as other than a perfect lady. But now... *was* she becoming a dried-up old maid? To be compared to Josephine Bassett!

She went to the mirror and studied her reflection anxiously. No, surely it was not so. Certainly her looks were not all she could wish, but she had begun to think they had improved lately, though she could not have said how. And the lines at the corners of her mouth were caused by laughter, were they not?

Trying to be as objective as possible, she decided that she was not like Alice's old-maid cousin. But what of the future? Might that be the direction in which she was headed? She shuddered at the thought, yet she *was* a spinster and very likely more set in her ways than she cared to think. And she was, perhaps, overly concerned with propriety. It would be difficult to change at this stage in her life, but, dear God, she did not wish to end up like Josephine Bassett.

Then another, happier thought struck her. She realized that she had already begun to change, so perhaps it would not be so very hard, after all. It was certain that she had relaxed her usual code of conduct with Jon. But, at the thought of Jon, she frowned again, fearing that, with him, she had allowed her behaviour to become a trifle *too* lax.

Her frown deepened as this train of thought brought to mind something he had said earlier.

Was he interested in Alice? It was certainly possible. As Jon had said, Alice was of marriageable age, and he was only three-and-thirty. Men of his age frequently married girls as young as she. Jane would not have thought a man of his stamp would be interested in marriage, but the fact that he had finally come to put Ethridge Hall to rights might be an indication that he had decided it was time to choose a wife and set up his nursery.

On the other hand, what if it were not marriage he had in mind? What if he meant to offer the girl a...a slip on the shoulder? But somehow she could not believe that Jon would behave in so base a way. He might be a demon with the ladies, but he would not stoop to seducing innocent young females. Still, for the time being, she had the girl under her care and therefore was responsible for protecting her.

Jane suddenly found herself wishing Alice at Jericho; anywhere but here. She knew jealousy was an unworthy emotion, and one to which she had no right, since she had no claim on Jon. But knowing a thing and doing something about it were very different.

Oh dear, what a muddle she was making.

Leaning towards her reflection in the mirror, she said aloud, "You foolish creature! You are behaving like a perfect ninnyhammer. It is time you stopped feeling sorry for yourself and began using some of the good sense you have always thought you possessed.''

Staring a moment longer, she added, ''And you are going to begin by getting rid of this useless object!'' She pulled the lacy cap from her head and flung it aside. She might be a spinster, but that did not mean she must go out of her way to look like one.

Feeling much better, she went to her wardrobe and began searching through her gowns for a more becoming one.

Striking a balance between all her opposing needs and desires would be something like walking a tightrope, but somehow she would manage. And with her new image, plus the return of her good sense, she was confident that she was equal to the challenges facing her.

CHAPTER NINE

As a FIRST STEP towards achieving her new goals, Jane went directly from her chamber to Alice's, determined to put things right between them—and not a moment too soon.

Alice, now dressed for travelling, was straining to close one of her bandboxes, which she had obviously packed herself, for the edge of a muslin garment could be seen poking out from under the recalcitrant lid. She looked up from her task with a guilty expression and said defiantly, "I am going to Brighton, to join Papa."

Refraining from asking how the girl intended to get there on her own, or how she thought she might manage with no more than could be stuffed into one bandbox, Jane said mildly, "How glad I am that I caught you in time then. Do you think we might talk for a few minutes before you go?"

"I suppose a few minutes will not matter, one way or the other," Alice conceded.

Jane stepped across the room and sat down on the side of the bed, then patted the place beside her. After a moment, Alice sat down next to her.

"Actually, I came to apologize to you," Jane told her.

"You did?" asked Alice, unable to hide her surprise.

"Indeed," said Jane. "What with St. Clair being here, and so ill, I fear I have been under a great deal of strain. As a result, you and I seem to have got off on the wrong foot. I was rather hoping we might change that and start anew."

Frowning slightly, Alice said slowly, "Well, I don't know. I don't think I wish to become a proper lady, after all. I know it is what Papa desires, but I do not see why I must change. Anyway," she added, "he will come round once he understands how much I dislike it."

Rather than answering that, Jane said, "Tell me, Alice. Do you wish for a London Season, and eventually, marriage?"

Looking shocked, the girl declared, "Of course! I certainly do not intend to be an old maid. But I don't see why I must learn all those stuffy rules in order to get a husband. I am very pretty. Everyone says so."

Inwardly wincing at such blatant conceit, as well as at her tactless remark, Jane calmly agreed. "Indeed, you are extremely pretty. And that might be enough, if you are not particular about who it is that you marry."

"What do you mean?" asked Alice suspiciously.

"Well, you are in possession of a very generous dowry. With that and your looks, you should have no trouble attaching a husband. I am sure there are any number of fortune-hunters in London who will not care a whit for how you conduct yourself.

"However," she continued, ignoring Alice's sudden frown, "it is unfortunate but true that gentlemen of the first consequence, when choosing a bride, tend to look for females who will not embarrass them by their behaviour. Although your beauty might attract them at first, in the end they will choose a true lady over a sad romp every time."

Alice's frown deepened, and after several long minutes, she said reluctantly, "Oh, very well. But must I spend every moment at those stupid lessons?"

Keeping all trace of victory from her voice, Jane said, "I don't suppose that is necessary, but you must spend *some* time at them."

Alice replied sulkily, "Yes, but Papa allowed me to bring Firefly, my mare, with me, and I have not even seen her since I arrived. I am used to riding her every day."

Really! The girl sounded as though she had been cooped up here for days. But Jane merely said, "I'll make a bargain with you, Alice. If you will agree to devote at least one hour in the morning and two in the afternoon to your lessons, I think we might give ourselves the treat of riding each morning before breakfast."

"Oh, capital!" cried Alice. "And St. Clair shall go with us."

"I fear that will not be possible," Jane told her quickly. "At least not for some time. You must remember that he has been very ill."

"Oh," said Alice, clearly disappointed. But then a sunny smile brightened her face. "But he will be able to go with us for our picnic on Saturday, will he not? We can take a carriage, so he needn't worry about riding.''

"Certainly he may, if he cares to.''

"Oh, he will,'' declared Alice with all the assurance of one who has seldom been denied anything. "I shall ask him.''

No longer feeling quite so kindly disposed towards the girl, Jane took her leave of Alice, who had already rung for her maid to come and unpack her bandbox.

Jane soon scolded herself out of her jealousy, although not without difficulty, and as she headed for the kitchen, she was even smiling a little. She was anticipating how St. Clair would laugh when he heard of her latest success in the art of bribery.

As it happened, however, she had no opportunity to speak privately with him during the next few days. She was called out several times to tend ill neighbours and since she had forbidden herself to go to his chamber, she saw him only at meals. In addition, when he was not resting, he was closeted in the estate room.

Had he truly been the highwayman, such a circumstance might have afforded her a great deal of gratification. As it was, she could only wonder what it was that he found so fascinating in a set of musty old account books.

It occurred to her that he seemed to be going out of his way to observe all the proprieties with her. She didn't know whether to be amused or vexed at such a turnabout, since it was he who had so often lured her into throwing caution to the wind before Alice's arrival.

But even had she gone against her better judgement and visited his room, she would not have been alone with him. The man, Kearny, whom she assumed to be his valet, had now become a member of the household and seemed always to be hovering protectively around his master.

By the time Saturday finally arrived, she was looking forward to their picnic almost as eagerly as Alice, for St. Clair had not only agreed to accompany them, but had declared that nothing could keep him from it. Even the knowledge that she would be sharing him with Alice could not dim Jane's pleasure at the thought of spending an hour or two with him in the relaxed atmosphere of such an outing.

Fortunately, St. Clair had sent for his own curricle, and they agreed to use it since Jane's was found to have a cracked axle. The day was far too lovely for them to be closed up in the carriage, which did not seem appropriate for such an excursion in any case. In fact, the picnic basket had already been packed and placed in St. Clair's vehicle when Melrose announced a caller.

Upon being told that the visitor was Mrs. Micklethorp, Jane was not only annoyed at this delay in their plans, but thoroughly surprised. The vicar's wife seldom troubled to make the journey all the way out to Meadowbrook. She enjoyed visiting with Jane and Agatha, but, being a trifle indolent, she preferred to let them come to her.

Jane feared that she knew the reason for this unprecedented visit, but she made her way to the drawing-room with as much polite composure as she could muster. She was all the more certain that she had guessed correctly when she saw Mrs. Micklethorp's forbidding countenance. Usually that lady was the most amiable of creatures, despite her penchant for gossip.

"My dear Jane," said Mrs. Micklethorp, scarcely giving her hostess time to shut the door. "I came as soon as I heard, and I must tell you that I was never so shocked in my life! You know how much I dislike interfering in other people's lives, but in this case, I feel that I should be neglecting my duty were I to remain silent."

While she drew breath to continue, Jane asked hastily, in the vain hope of postponing the inevitable, "Would you care for some tea, Mrs. Micklethorp?"

"No, no!" said that lady. Then, "Well, perhaps just one cup, and possibly one or two of those delicious little cakes your cook is so good at making."

Jane walked to the bell-pull, but her guest was not to be put off. She said, "But you must not try to divert me from my purpose, Jane."

Sighing, Jane moved to a nearby chair and reluctantly prepared to hear the woman out. "I collect you have not come merely for a visit. And that being so, what is your purpose, Mrs. Micklethorp?"

"I think you know that very well, my dear, but in case you do not—Jane, how *could* you take that man into your home and allow him to run tame here for an entire sennight? And, if what I hear is true, he is *still* here!"

"If you are referring to Lord St. Clair," said Jane with cool civility, "I had little choice in the matter. He was inadvertently shot by my own coachman, so naturally I felt responsible. And since he needed immediate care, and Meadowbrook was so close, it seemed the most reasonable thing to do."

"So I was told and, knowing you as I do, I would think nothing of it were he anyone else. But, my dear, you *know* his reputation."

"Certainly I know that he has one, although no one has ever bothered to tell me just what he has done to deserve it."

"Well," declared Mrs. Micklethorp, colouring, "for one thing, he is a notorious libertine. And, though you know little of the world despite your years, I am sure you know what *that* means."

"Oh yes," said Jane, her smile forced. "I believe the term refers to a man who is noted for his many—" she cast about in her mind for the proper word "—light o'loves. But from the little I *do* know of the world, in that way he is very much like many gentlemen of the ton. The only difference is that he is more open and honest about his affairs."

Jane was feeling all the dismay and mortification she would have expected to feel at finding herself in a position to be lectured to and gossiped about. What she had not expected, however, was to feel such anger and indignation. But she thought she could safely say that she knew St. Clair better, by now, than Mrs.

Micklethorp or any other of her neighbours. And she could not meekly allow him to be attacked in this way.

Mrs. Micklethorp's colour had risen even higher, and she said, "I see that this is more serious than I feared. He has already begun corrupting you."

Seeing how alarmingly red her guest's face had become, and fearing she might be in danger of suffering an apoplexy, Jane decided that conciliation would serve her better than anger. Leaning forward earnestly, she said, "Dear Mrs. Micklethorp, I know that your intentions are of the best and that you speak only out of concern for me, but I assure you that the viscount has not corrupted me. Far from it! I have found him to be most..." She wanted to say "gentlemanly" but found she could not quite manage that. Instead, she lamely substituted, "Likeable and charming."

"Oh, yes. I do not doubt that. Charm, after all, is a rake's stock in trade," said Mrs. Micklethorp scathingly. Then with an air of martyrdom, she continued, "Well, I see there is no help for it. I must tell you the whole truth about him, no matter how distasteful it is to me. You are a maiden lady, Jane, and no one has wished to sully your ears with such a sordid tale. But if that is the only way to bring you to your senses, I must not permit a concern for delicacy to stand in my way."

Ever since she had first begun hearing of St. Clair, Jane had wondered what he could have done to earn such a reputation. She knew there was more to it than just the fact that he was a rake. During her one Season, she had discovered that London was well populated with rakes, most of whom were accepted into the first circles of Society.

At least they were accepted so long as they were reasonably discreet about their peccadilloes, which, apparently, St. Clair was not. But, even so, the ton, particularly the ladies, had a certain peculiar fondness for the breed, and it was they who ruled Society.

But now that she was about to be told the real reason for St. Clair's ostracism, she found herself extremely reluctant to hear it. Where the devil was Melrose with that tea? she wondered crossly as Mrs. Micklethorp leaned forward to say with ill-concealed relish, "It happened many years ago, of course, although his youth cannot excuse what he did. I shall not mention the young lady's name, but I assure you, she came of an excellent family, and St. Clair—"

At that moment, there came a scratching at the door, followed by Melrose's entrance with the tea tray. Jane was so grateful that she could have embraced him. She was even more gratified when Agatha entered the room on his heels.

Her face wreathed in smiles, Agatha sailed across the room to seat herself beside the visitor. "My dear Mrs. Micklethorp," she said. "What a pleasant surprise this is. You have not visited us in ages."

"No," said that lady in a rather disconcerted manner. "Well, as the vicar's wife, I have many obligations, you know. And I see you so often when you visit Dunby that there is no need— But I did wish to have a word with Jane."

"Very thoughtful of you," said Agatha, beginning to pour the tea. Then, after handing their guest a cup, she looked at Jane. "Should you not be leaving now, Jane? You are already quite late for your appointment."

"Oh, yes," said Jane, rising hastily. "Please excuse me, Mrs. Micklethorp. I do appreciate your concern and I assure you that I shall think about what you have said. But I have promised this time to young Alice Brant, and I cannot disappoint her."

The vicar's wife opened her mouth, but before she could speak, Agatha said, "Now you just run along, love, and do not worry about us. Mrs. Micklethorp and I shall manage nicely on our own and enjoy a comfortable coze."

Jane wasted not a moment in taking her advice. Just before closing the drawing-room door behind her, she heard Agatha saying, "Now, you must try one of these new cakes Cook has made. I know you are partial to her others, but this is a new recipe, and..."

Leaning her forehead against the cool wood of the door, Jane released her breath in a small puff of laughter. Poor Mrs. Micklethorp was no match for Agatha. Once her companion set her mind to it, she could outmanoeuvre and out-gossip even the most accomplished tale-tattler.

She turned, then, to find St. Clair watching her from across the entry hall with answering laughter in his eyes.

He said, "It is about time! I was beginning to think I would be obliged to come and rescue you myself."

Jane smiled. "I don't think that would have been a good notion. I am afraid our vicar's wife has a rather unflattering opinion of you."

He looked at her sharply but merely said, "Been blackening my character, has she?"

"No more than usual," said Jane lightly. Then, looking round, she asked, "But where is Alice?"

"Outside, champing at the bit," he replied. "So you had best step lively, my girl."

"Oh, my, yes. Just let me get my bonnet and I shall be ready."

Outside, Jane was somewhat surprised to find Alice mounted on her mare, and more than a little pleased at the thought that just she and St. Clair would be sharing the curricle. She had been wondering how the three of them would manage in a vehicle meant to seat only two comfortably.

There was no question of her being private with him, however, as Alice chose to ride beside the carriage, chattering and flirting outrageously with him most of the time. For all that, Jane was content, speaking only now and then to give directions.

It was one of those idyllic summer days, sunny and warm, with a hint of a breeze. The sky was incredibly blue, dotted here and there with fluffy white clouds wherein one could see all manner of fantastic and magical shapes.

Jane drew a deep breath and marvelled that she had never before been so acutely conscious of the myriad and delightful smells of summertime in Yorkshire. But most of all, she was aware of the man beside her, whose scent was so peculiarly his own, and somehow, more pleasing than all the rest.

It did not take them long to arrive at the location Jane had chosen for their outing, a grassy glade beside a small stream. St. Clair glanced round as he handed her down from the curricle, and remarked, "Correct me if I am wrong, but is this not part of my property?"

"Oh dear, you have caught me out. But I must own that I have been trespassing here for a good many years—since long before it was your property. It is one of my favourite places, and I doubt the former owner ever knew of my crime. Are you going to exact a fine from me?"

His eyes gleaming with amusement, he replied, "No, not in a monetary sense. All the same, I think I must claim some sort of forfeit from you."

But Jane was left to wonder what that might be.

Upon their arrival, Alice had jumped down from her horse without waiting for assistance, and after securing the reins to a nearby bush, she had begun exploring the glade. There was little to interest her, however, and now she was back, demanding, "A forfeiture for what?"

"For trespassing on my land," St. Clair told her.

"Oh, is this your land? I had not realized it was such a vast estate. Was that old curmudgeon a relative of yours? Papa says he was as rich as Croesus, so you must be very plump in the pocket now. I suppose that will make you a great deal more acceptable to the ton, will it not?"

Jane had to clench her jaw to keep from criticizing the girl, but she was determined not to spoil this day by sending Alice into a temper. To salve her conscience, she told herself that she would find a way later to bring up the subject diplomatically.

St. Clair, however, was looking decidedly as though he were ready to give Alice a severe set-down. Meeting Jane's eyes, however, he seemed to understand the pleading in them. He turned back to Alice and said mildly, "It *is* my land, and the old gentleman was a relative, although a very distant one. I have no notion of how my inheritance will affect the ton's view of me, and it is impolite to enquire into a man's wealth, or lack thereof... unless you are the father of a marriageable daughter."

Jane held her breath, expecting a tantrum, but to her surprise, Alice merely said, "Oh." Then, with an abrupt change of subject, she asked, "May we eat now? We were late in starting, and I am famished."

There was no opportunity for private talk during the picnic meal, but on the trip back to Meadowbrook, Alice did not remain quite so close to the carriage. Jane guessed that the girl was a little out of charity with St. Clair, for he had treated her with amused tolerance all morning. Now, bored and restless since the promised treat was over, Alice had apparently decided to punish him by depriving him of her company. She took to galloping ahead of them, then waiting impatiently for them to catch up before forging ahead again.

Watching her, and hoping she would not be so imprudent as to go beyond their sight, Jane said ruefully, "I suppose I should arrange some entertainments for her and invite the other young people from the neighbourhood to keep her amused."

Glancing at her with a grin, St. Clair said dryly, "Forgive me, Jane, but I am heartily sick of the chit and her problems. I don't wish to talk of her."

"Oh, of course not. I did not mean to bore you with my troubles."

"Your troubles do not bore me. It is simply that I would rather speak of other things just now. For instance, I have not told you how glad I am that you have left off wearing those ridiculous caps. You are far too young and attractive for such things."

Jane wished with all her heart that she did not blush so easily. She said in a slightly strangled voice, "Oh, well, Agatha is forever scolding me for wearing them. I simply grew tired of listening to her. But there is no need to offer me Spanish coin. I am neither young nor particularly attractive."

"You are younger, by several years, than I," he told her. "As to the other, perhaps it is true that beauty is in the eye of the beholder."

It was a good thing that he was not watching her then, for she was certain that her absurd happiness at his compliment showed clearly on her face. Even the knowledge that he must be very practised at making such speeches could not dampen the thrill she felt. Sincere or not, she knew she would cherish his words forever.

They were silent for several minutes then, and her thoughts returned to Mrs. Micklethorp and what she had been about to reveal. What terrible thing would she have learned about St. Clair if they had not been interrupted? She did not want to know, yet she could not stop wondering.

She could not have known that St. Clair's thoughts were on the same subject, but, just as they turned into the carriage drive at Meadowbrook, he said, "Jane, I need to speak with you. Not now, for what I have to say to you is private. Will you agree to meet with me later?"

Without stopping to consider, she answered, "I shall come to your chamber tonight."

"No!" he said sharply. Then, gentling his tone, he repeated, "No. That would not be wise. Besides, Kearny is certain to be somewhere within earshot. It would be better if we met in the rose garden after Alice is abed."

"Very well," she agreed quietly, pleased at how calm she sounded when, in truth, she felt oddly excited and rather daring at the thought of such an assignation with St. Clair. What could he mean to tell her?

If he was going to divulge the truth about himself, she preferred to hear it from him rather than from someone else. But perhaps it was something else altogether . . .

CHAPTER TEN

BY THE TIME they arrived at the front entrance, Alice had already disappeared in the direction of the stables, and after handing Jane down from the curricle, St. Clair drove off in that direction, too. Jane watched, bemused, until he was out of sight, then turned towards the house.

With her thoughts wholly centred upon the proposed rendezvous with St. Clair later that night, she wondered how she would manage to get through the intervening hours. But all of that flew from her head when she stepped through the door to discover a state of near pandemonium.

Elsie stood near the bottom of the stairs, glaring at Melrose. At the sight of her mistress, she cried, "It weren't my fault! Melrose weren't nowhere about, and how was I to know the old cat—I mean the vicar's wife—can't abide the squire?"

Before Jane could enquire as to the meaning of this astounding speech, Melrose answered sharply, "If you had but waited a moment, instead of rushing to answer the door yourself—which you know well is no part of your duties—I should have been here. Now, if you know what is good for you, you will stop bothering Miss Jane and take yourself off to the kitchen to help Cook."

The maid flounced away. Melrose turned to his mistress to offer his own apologies, but Jane scarcely heard him or registered his unusually harassed look.

Alice and St. Clair had just come in, but her attention was riveted on the sound of a booming male voice coming from the drawing-room. "Here now, woman, be careful with that foot. It hurts like the very devil!"

Agatha's voice sounded unsympathetic. "Oh, stop your complaining, Alfred. You have only yourself to blame. If you were not forever attempting to behave as if you were still a young blade..."

"Papa!" shrieked Alice, and dashing past Jane, she flew into the drawing-room.

"Ah, there you are, puss. Come give your papa a kiss, but be careful of that foot."

St. Clair raised his eyebrows at Jane and said, "I believe this is a case where retreat is the better part of valour. I shall be in the estate room should you need me."

Jane merely nodded distractedly and went to the drawing-room. There she discovered Sir Alfred, sitting in a wing-chair beside the empty fireplace fondly greeting his daughter, while Agatha finished arranging his heavily bandaged left foot on a pillow-topped footstool.

"Sir Alfred!" Jane said, wondering if she sounded as stupid as she feared she did. "I thought you would be in Brighton, or on your way to the Continent by now."

"Aye, and so I should have been, had it not been for this," he growled, nodding at the offending appendage. "But I must have injured the damned toe somehow, for the confounded thing has swelled like a blasted balloon and is devilish painful."

"In a pig's eye!" said Agatha inelegantly. "Injured, indeed! It is the gout, and comes as a result of all that rich food and drink, not to mention other things which are better left unsaid. And I shall thank you to keep a civil tongue in your head while you are in this house, sir!"

Jane thought she heard Agatha add, "Old fool," under her breath, but could not be certain.

After favouring Agatha with a blistering scowl, the squire looked sheepishly at Jane and apologized for his language, then said, "But what is this I hear about St. Clair?"

"Oh, Papa!" declared Alice. "Only think, I have been staying in the same house as a noted rake!" Then she added with a slight pout, "But he is not at all what I thought he would be. In fact, he treats me as though he were my uncle, or some such thing."

Looking somewhat relieved, Sir Alfred said, "Well, well. Always liked the fellow myself, even if he is a bounder. Hear he has inherited everything from that old curmudgeon Caldwell, though, so I expect all that nasty business will soon be forgiven. Even so, can't have him living in the same house as my young puss, here."

For the briefest of moments, Jane was sorely tempted to tell him that he might take his daughter away with him, with her blessing. But of course she could not be so uncivil. Instead, thinking it time to take command of the situation, she sent a reluctant Alice off to change out of her riding habit, then told Sir Alfred, "Your daughter, sir, is being well chaperoned. And as for St. Clair, he has been recuperating here after an unfortunate accident. Ethridge Hall, as you know, is scarcely fit for occupancy."

"Well, well," said the squire again with a thoughtful frown. "No doubt you are right. Might not be such a bad thing for my girl, after all. Hear he has hired workmen to set the Hall to rights, which makes me wonder if he is planning to mend his ways and settle down. By all accounts he is rich as a nabob now. Before we know it, all the matchmaking mamas will be throwing their eligible daughters in his path. No harm in my puss having a head start, is there?"

Jane had no notion of how to answer that remarkable speech. *So much for taking command of the situation,* she thought wryly.

She turned at the sound of someone clearing his throat and found Melrose still standing in the doorway. "Yes, Melrose?" she asked.

"I was wondering, Miss Jane, what you wished me to do about the lady."

"The lady?"

"The vicar's wife."

"Good God!" Jane exclaimed. "Is she still here?"

"I am afraid so, Miss Jane. She was a trifle overset when the squire arrived, and—"

"Ha!" interpolated Sir Alfred. "That's rich! 'A trifle overset.' Went into a spasm is what she did."

"I had her removed to the morning-room," finished Melrose rather faintly.

"Damned gossiping busybody," muttered Sir Alfred.

"Great heavens!" declared Agatha. "I forgot all about her. You had better go to her, Jane. I could not get rid of her, for she is determined to speak to you, and I fear she won't leave until she does. I have a fair notion of what it is she means to tell you." Then she added rather cryptically, "Just remember that there is always more than one way to look at a thing."

Squelching a pudding-hearted urge to feign illness, Jane said, "Very well," and walked resolutely from the room.

As she mounted the stairs, she heard Sir Alfred saying, "Speaking of unfortunate accidents, did you hear that I was robbed by that devilish rogue of a highwayman? And the damned fellow is still on the loose. Don't know what this world is coming to!"

Jane did not hear Agatha's reply, nor did the thought of the highwayman bother her any longer. In any event, she had too many other things on her mind. A few moments later, she entered the morning-room with a determined smile pasted on her lips.

Mrs. Micklethorp was lying on the sofa, clutching a vinaigrette in her hand, but at Jane's entrance, she sat up and looked at her accusingly. "Praise God, you have finally returned," she said. "I don't know how much longer I could bear to remain under the same roof as that man."

"St. Clair?" Jane was surprised into asking. So far as she knew, the lady had not so much as laid eyes on St. Clair.

"No, no, not St. Clair—well, him, too, but I was referring, on this occasion, to Squire Brant. The man has an evil tongue in his head and not an ounce of civility in his body. As you know, my dear, a vicar's wife must deal with a great many persons of the lower classes, but they, at least, know how to show a proper respect. Such language as he uses! Well! As I said, I could scarcely bear to remain in the same house with him."

Suppressing a strong inclination to tell her persistent guest that no one had constrained her to do so, Jane said, "I'm sorry, but I had no notion that you would stay for such a lo—I mean I had not realized that you meant to wait for me, ma'am."

"I know my duty, Jane, and as I told you earlier, I came to speak with you and I mean to do so before I go."

As much as Jane had longed to avoid this, she now only wished for the woman to say her piece and leave. In any case, it appeared that nothing would stop her.

Deciding that it was better to hear the truth now, rather than indulge in speculation, Jane sat down wearily. "Very well, ma'am. Just what *is* it that St. Clair is supposed to have done?"

Mrs. Micklethorp assumed the classic pose of someone about to offer a choice morsel of gossip, while at the same time managing to appear reluctant.

Even as she wondered at such an ability, Jane resigned herself to hearing a long, involved tale.

However, the vicar's wife told the whole in only two sentences. She said, not entirely unsympathetically, "I fear there is no supposing about it, for the story came from the most reliable source. In any event, not to wrap the matter in clean linen, my dear, he eloped with a young lady, got her with child, then abandoned her to her fate, refusing to marry her."

Surprised by the brevity of that speech, and shocked by its content, Jane's first inclination was to deny that it could be true. But something stopped her. She could not, however, think of any other response, and so she watched in a silent daze as her guest rose, saying, "There, I have done what I came to do. I shall go now, but I do hope that you will consider well all that I have said, and act accordingly."

With that, Mrs. Micklethorp took her leave, but Jane scarcely registered that she was finally gone.

What she had heard was far worse than anything she had imagined. For him to have abandoned the girl after getting her with child . . . no, she could not believe that of him. And yet, even loving gossip as the vicar's wife did, would she repeat such a vicious tale if it were completely unsubstantiated?

Jane hated the doubt which had insinuated itself into her mind, but could not rid herself of it.

Mrs. Micklethorp had said that the story came from the most reliable source, which could only be the girl or her family. But surely they would not have wished to broadcast such a disaster. They would be more likely to do all in their power to hush it up, would they not?

By now, Jane's head was throbbing and she longed for nothing so much as the privacy of her own chamber, where she could try to come to terms with her confused feelings. For, even while she unhappily accepted the possible—probable?—truth of the story, she was desperately trying to find excuses for St. Clair.

But she could not do as she wished; she still had a guest to see to. It would be too uncivil to ignore the squire's presence in such a way, and so she forced herself to return to the drawing-room.

On her way, a new concern occurred to her. She knew that Sir Alfred had given most of his staff leave, since he had expected to be away for some time. What if she were obliged to house him, too? Her financial resources were already considerably strained.

In the end, she was not obliged to house the squire. He did, however, accept her invitation to stay for dinner, which turned out to be both a blessing and a trial. It was a severe strain to sit at table with St. Clair and attempt to behave as if nothing had changed when, in fact, her heart was breaking. It was fortunate, therefore, that the squire was there, for he dominated the conversation, making her inability to meet St. Clair's eyes, or to speak easily with him, less obvious.

Afterwards, as St. Clair said good-night, he gave her a meaningful look and, under his breath, murmured, "Until later."

She knew he was referring to their proposed meeting in the garden, but she could not tell him that she would not be there. For one thing, they were not alone, and for another, she did not know what to say to him. More to the point, she feared she might burst into tears if she tried to speak.

In her chamber, as she slowly made ready for bed, she wondered dejectedly how long he would wait for her. Not long, she thought. During dinner, Mrs. Micklethorp's extended visit had been mentioned, and St. Clair had looked at Jane sharply. His understanding was highly acute, so no doubt he already suspected that she now knew the truth about him and would not be surprised by her failure to appear.

Perhaps he would even be gone by the time she awakened in the morning. And she wondered, as she crawled into bed, why that thought should make her weep.

CHAPTER ELEVEN

ST. CLAIR WAITED for Jane for scarcely a quarter of an hour. She knew this because she had frequently glanced at the clock by her bedside. So she knew exactly what time it was when her door opened and he strode into her chamber.

The sight of him filled her with such happiness that, just for a moment, she forgot all other considerations. Yet somehow this seemed much more improper than *her* visits to *his* chamber had ever been.

Sitting up, Jane clutched the sheet to her chest and hissed, "St. Clair! What are you doing here?"

He neither spoke nor stopped until he was standing beside her bed. Then, arms akimbo, he glared down at her and said, "If Mohammed will not come to the mountain... But I think I know why you failed to keep our appointment. It was the vicar's wife, was it not? Mrs. Middlethrop?"

"Micklethorp," she corrected as she turned her head away, not wishing him to see how reddened her eyes must be, and feeling unaccountably ashamed for having failed him.

But he took her chin in his hand and turned it back. "No, do not turn away from me. We are going to have this out now, though why I should care— In any event, the lady told you a most unsavoury tale about me, did she not? And you not only believed her, but have already judged me."

"No, but—oh, I don't know what to believe!" Jane cried in agitation.

"Hush," he said, "or the entire household will hear us."

Stung by his criticism, she nevertheless lowered her voice as she replied indignantly, "It seems very strange to find you so aware of propriety. Before I met you I would not have dreamed of being so indiscreet."

Amusement leapt into his eyes at that, and he said, "*Mea culpa*. You see, I admit my fault." Then, becoming sober once more, he added, "But this is the very height of indiscretion, and should we be discovered, we should certainly find ourselves in the suds. Your reputation would be as damaged as my own. And it was you who once told me that Society can be cruel to those who do not heed its rules, though, God knows, I have reason enough of my own to know that."

"Yes," she said quietly. "As do I."

As though he had not heard her, he continued, "Which is all the more reason why I should not have encouraged you to go against those rules."

"Oh, no," she told him truthfully, "you cannot take all the blame. I am not a child to be so easily led. You could not have influenced me had I not— But if you fear discovery, perhaps you should go now."

"Not just yet. I doubt that anyone will learn of this meeting if we are careful, and I have yet to tell you what I came to say. Are you willing to listen to my version of what happened all those years ago?"

Suddenly recalling Agatha's saying that there was more than one way to see a thing, Jane reconsidered. Though the evidence against him seemed quite overwhelming, perhaps he would be able to exonerate himself. Besides, his words recalled to her the fact that all this was rather ancient history; he could not have been much more than a youth at the time.

With those thoughts, hope rose in her breast, and she found that she was not only willing, but ridiculously eager to hear his version of the story.

However, she managed to keep her voice and expression calm as she replied, "Of course. I hope I am not so closed-minded that I would refuse such a request."

He smiled and murmured, "Good girl," before saying, "When I asked you to meet with me tonight, I had meant to tell the tale then. If you were to learn the truth about me—and I knew that sooner or later you must—I preferred that you hear it from me. I suppose I should have told you sooner, but..." He stopped, walked a few steps away, then abruptly came back. "Damnation, I am finding this more difficult than I thought, and it may take some time."

Jane merely nodded, and St. Clair sat down on the edge of her bed. He was silent for a while, but finally he began to speak. "After I came down from Oxford, I was quite mad for purchasing a pair of colours and going off to war, but, as I was the only son, my father naturally opposed that notion. I, of course, did not see it as natural at the time. I could not even conceive of being killed. At that age, one tends to think of oneself as immortal, I suppose. Even so, I had a cousin who was next in line for the title, so it was not as if he had no other heir.

"My father and I quarrelled bitterly, which was not unusual for us, and I took myself off to London, where I set up my bachelor's establishment and went my length to put my father's back up at every opportunity."

He smiled faintly. "Oh, I thought I was quite the buck, top-of-the-trees, awake on every suit. And, oddly enough, I was, in most cases. Or perhaps I had a guardian angel looking over my shoulder. At least I managed to avoid most of the pitfalls awaiting young greenhorns on their own in London for the first time. But I found that I was not awake in all cases."

He fell silent again. Jane waited for him to continue, but she was no longer quite so tense. She could so easily see him as the young man he described, disappointed in his desire to go to war, then going off to London to prove himself. She was smiling slightly at this picture of him when he spoke again.

"One day I received a visit from a young lady whom I'd known all my life, although I had not seen her for several years. She was a year or two older than I, but we'd grown up together on neighbouring estates, and I had always considered her a friend. She told me that she was being forced into marriage with a man who was old enough to be her grandfather. He was not only physically repulsive to her, but she feared him because she'd heard rumours of his cruelty to his first wife. She pleaded with me to save her.''

"But," interrupted Jane, "were her parents the sort who would do that to their daughter? I know such things used to be quite common, but it sounds very gothic in this day and age.''

"Yes, and I would not have thought her parents capable of such insensitivity. They had always doted upon her, in fact. But I had heard that her father was in dun territory, and her story was very convincing. In addition, she was clearly distraught. In any case, she had already ruined herself by running away from home and by coming to a bachelor's rooms alone, and so there was only one thing I could see to do. I agreed to elope with her.''

Jane could not agree that elopement had been the best solution, but she could certainly understand why he might have thought so at the time. Nevertheless, she began to feel rather tense again.

She had been hoping that he would deny the whole story, but so far, his version, although more detailed, did not diverge overmuch from Mrs. Micklethorp's. He had admitted to running off with the girl, and she dreaded hearing that the rest was also true.

He must have felt or sensed the change in her, for he lifted a brow in enquiry.

"I am not certain that I wish to hear the remainder of this," she said, only half meaning it.

"A pity," he answered grimly. "But you agreed to listen, and you shall hear it." He studied her silently for a moment, then asked, "What is it that has you flying into the boughs? The elopement? I know it is quite scandalous, but it would have been forgotten in time."

"Would it?" she asked, surprising even herself with the amount of bitterness she felt as she was suddenly reminded of her mother's elopement and its repercussions.

"Why are you reacting this way?"

He sounded genuinely puzzled, and Jane bit her lip as she considered his question. *Was* she reacting excessively? After a few minutes of inner struggle, she was forced to admit that she might be.

Shaking her head, she said, "It is nothing. I fear I am not very rational when it comes to— But you were quite young at the time, were you not? And you must have been caught before you could marry—at least, you didn't marry her, did you?"

"Oh, no," he answered sardonically.

"I am surprised that her parents did not simply condone your marriage once they caught up with you. That way, the scandal would have been forgotten more quickly, or even prevented entirely. But I suppose the other man was much wealthier than you." Jane sighed and shook her head again. "I would not have thought, however, that he would still want the poor girl after that. What happened? Were they able to keep word of the elopement from him until after they were wed?"

St. Clair gave the most cynical laugh Jane had ever heard. "My dear, you have not heard the worst. We were not caught at all. It was I who took her back to her parents and told them I wished them joy of her."

"Good God!" exclaimed Jane, turning pale and staring at him. She was certain now that he was not going to deny any part of the tale, and she imagined the worst. Still, she felt she must know it all before she could judge him. She leaned towards him and asked, "What happened?"

Her attention caught up in his story, Jane had forgotten to hold the sheet up before her, and now St. Clair tore his gaze from where the soft lawn of her gown clearly showed the shape of her breasts. Clearing his throat, he said, "Yes, well, to continue my story, the journey from London to Gretna Green is a long one, and I soon discovered that I did not know the young lady nearly so well as I had thought. She turned out to be the Devil's own daughter, and before we'd gone halfway, we were at daggers drawn.

"Finally, one night, in the midst of screaming invective at me, she let it be known how she had taken me in. Everything she had told me was a lie. There was no forced marriage to a repulsive old man. In truth, she had run away because she'd been intimate with the head groom and was now carrying his child. She had hit upon me as a likely candidate to be the babe's father. That was when I took her home to her parents.

"Of course she thought she had me well and truly trapped, and when she found just how mistaken she was, she took her revenge by insisting to her parents that I was, indeed, the father. Needless to say, they believed her."

"Oh dear," said Jane. She knew that sounded woefully inadequate, but she was so relieved she scarcely knew what she was saying.

He laughed. "Indeed. Overnight, I found myself an outcast from Society as well as disowned by my father."

"And I suppose you were too full of pride to try to defend yourself," she said quietly.

"What! And further damage the lady's reputation? But to be truthful, I did try to explain the matter to my father, though I might just as well have saved my breath. When even *he* believed that I had ravished the girl, got her with child, and refused to marry her, I decided that he and Society could go to the Devil. I caught the first ship leaving port, which happened to be bound for America."

For all his flippancy, she knew how hurt he must have been, and also that he would not welcome any expression of sympathy. Instead, she said, "Well! I do not blame you in the least."

"Ah, but had I been a true gentleman—and I am the first to admit that I am not—I would have married her and made the best of it."

She wrinkled her nose. "Perhaps, but had you done so, you both would have ended by being utterly miserable, and I doubt there *was* a best to be made of it. I feel sorry for the girl, but she brought her own troubles upon herself and should not have attempted to drag you into it. No, had I been in your shoes, I would not have married her, either. And only think of the marvellous adventures which you would not otherwise have had.''

"Oh, Jane," he said, the laughter back in his eyes, "you are a pearl beyond price."

"And you are an outrageous flatterer," she retorted.

He only shook his head, and after a few minutes, she said, "I suppose you should be going. It must be very late."

"Not yet," he said, and put his hand on her arm as though she were the one needing to be detained. "I have told you my sorry tale, and now I am curious about yours. Why is it that you can accept what most people consider the unforgivable about me, yet you flew into the boughs when I first mentioned elopement? That is what set you off, is it not?"

Jane stared down at her hands, wishing that she had not aroused his curiosity by behaving so foolishly earlier. "I'm sorry," she murmured, "but, as I said, I am not very rational on that subject."

He said nothing, but was obviously waiting for her to continue.

With a deep sigh, she said, "It was not so much the mention of your elopement which set me off, but your remark that it would eventually be forgotten. You see, my mother eloped with another man so I, too, know what it is to be in the midst of a scandal. And I have learned that where scandal is concerned, Society can have a very long memory indeed."

"Ahh" was all he said.

Jane straightened, and lifted her chin, deciding that since she had come this far, she might as well tell him the whole. "My father ranted and raved, calling her all manner of horrible names...well, she had always been rather frivolous and fun-loving and a trifle careless of propriety. In any event, I made up my mind, that day, to be all that she was not. I thought that if no one could say that I was like her in any way, I could somehow protect myself, and my father would— But he only became more reclusive and irascible. By the time I realized that it was not going to make a difference, being the proper Miss Lockwood had become a way of life for me."

She suddenly gave a forced little laugh. "Do you know, I have never spoken of this before. Not even with Agatha."

"Why? It might have been better for you if you had."

"I suppose because it was too painful and I was too ashamed." She tried to sound detached but could not entirely keep the remembered anguish from her voice.

"Now what is this?" he asked. "Why should you feel shame for what your mother did?"

With a lightness she did not feel, she said, "Oh, it is silly, I know, but I have always felt that if I had been more what she wished for in a daughter—prettier or perhaps more lovable—she would not have left."

"My foolish girl," he said, holding her by the shoulders and giving her a small shake, "that is the greatest piece of nonsense I have ever heard. It seems to me that if anyone was to blame, other than your mother, it was your father. He sounds as if he was a very disagreeable man, and the two of them mismatched."

Jane stared at him for a moment, wondering why such a reasonable explanation for her mother's defection had never occurred to her. But then, she had always been too busy blaming herself to have seen such an obvious truth. One should not think ill of the dead, but to say that her father had been disagreeable was understating the matter.

With a small laugh, she said, "Do you know, I believe you are right. You were right about something else, too. I do feel much better for having spoken of this."

"Exactly so!" he said with a grin.

In truth, Jane felt as light as a feather, as though a great weight had suddenly been lifted from her. And, without thinking, she impulsively scrambled to her knees, threw her arms about his neck, and said fervently, "Thank you!"

Afterwards, she could not have related the exact progression of events, but she did remember that his arms had tightened around her, and then she was lying back on the bed with St. Clair beside her, his mouth descending towards hers. And all those fluttering sensations were back in her chest and stomach, but she no longer thought of them as the least bit unpleasant.

Far from protesting, she raised her own head eagerly to meet him—and their noses bumped.

With a small huff of laughter, he said, "Tilt your head a little, sweetheart."

She did, and his mouth moulded to hers perfectly. She was enjoying it very much and was only a little surprised when his tongue began teasing the seam of her lips, but she was more than willing to enjoy that, too. And when he raised his head slightly and murmured, "Open your mouth for me, dearest," she did so without a thought for propriety.

In fact, Jane was thinking very little. All her awareness was of the wonderful, marvellous sensations he was creating in her body with his mouth and hands. She felt as though she had made a momentous discovery, and if she thought at all, it was to wonder if anyone else had ever experienced this astounding thing. And if they had, why had it been kept such a secret?

As he kissed her, his right hand had been caressing her arm and shoulder. Now it moved to her side and slid slowly down to her hip before moving upwards again with that same tantalizing slowness. It stopped just below her breast, and Jane held her breath, knowing that she wanted him to touch her there more than anything in the world.

But he did not. Instead, he suddenly stiffened and pulled away from her with a muttered curse, then stood and ran his hands through his hair.

Confused, and feeling cold and bereft at his abrupt withdrawal, Jane stammered, "I—I'm sorry. I . . ."

Glancing back with a harsh laugh, he said, "Not nearly so sorry as I. That should never have happened, but at least you have learned a valuable lesson. You see, now, what comes of consorting with a rake."

Jane was very glad, a moment later, that she stifled the protest that rose to her lips, for as he turned away again, he said, "To think that I would attempt to seduce even *you!*"

Had he slapped her face, she could not have been more shocked, but nothing could have brought her to her senses more effectively. She said coldly, "I think you had better leave now."

"Yes," he agreed, and strode to the door.

Unable to look at him, she stared straight ahead as she listened to the door open, then waited to hear it close. But, when it did not, she finally turned her head to see him gazing at her.

He said, "Jane, I..." He stopped and shook his head as if he would say something, but instead he turned abruptly and left her room.

Jane found herself alone to suffer the sting of rejection, as well as self-disgust, knowing that nothing would have occurred had she not thrown herself at him so brazenly. She also knew that, had he not found the attempted seduction of her too distasteful to continue, she would have done nothing to stop him. She was forced to the bitter realization that she was her mother's daughter, after all.

Over and over, as she lay sleepless in her bed, her mind replayed the events of the past hour while she wished with all her heart that she could somehow change them. And, over and over, she wondered how she was going to face St. Clair in the morning.

CHAPTER TWELVE

AS IT HAPPENED, when morning finally arrived, Jane discovered that her worries had been for nothing. When she entered the breakfast room, she found only Agatha and Alice there. She could not prevent her eyes from going to the empty chair where St. Clair usually sat.

Agatha, who had been watching her closely, said baldly, "He is gone."

"Gone?"

"St. Clair," Agatha explained. "He and that odd man of his have taken themselves off to Ethridge Hall."

"Oh," said Jane, going to her chair and trying desperately to hide her devastation. She yearned to ask if they had gone to stay at Ethridge Hall or if they had merely gone to inspect it. But she dared not, for fear of revealing too much.

Her question, however, was answered when Alice sighed and said, "It will be very dull here without him, even though he is not nearly so dashing as I thought he would be. But I daresay we shall see him quite often, since the Hall is so close by."

For a moment, Jane felt the beginnings of hope, but in the next, despair descended again. They would not see him unless it came about by accident. She had seen to that by her actions last night. She had not only given him a disgust of her, but had ruined all chances for any sort of relationship between them—even that of friendship.

Agatha said with exaggerated nonchalance, "He said that since the Hall was now habitable, there was no longer any need to take advantage of your hospitality. I thought it very peculiar that he should leave so abruptly and without the least notice, but I suppose he had his reasons. Oh, and he asked me to thank you—for everything."

Jane merely nodded and forced herself to feign interest in the food on her plate.

Blithely unaware of the emotional undertones in the air, Alice unwittingly came to Jane's rescue by changing the subject, although the new one was only slightly more welcome. She said, "I can scarce wait till tomorrow! I have not been to Leeds in an age!"

Having completely forgotten her promise to take Alice to Leeds on Monday, Jane was at first filled with dismay. At the moment, she could think of nothing she wished less to do. But on second thought, she decided that it might be the very thing for her. She needed to keep busy so that she would not have time for moping. But today was Sunday, which was customarily the slowest day of the week, and she still must get through it somehow.

Immediately after church and a cold nuncheon, she was summoned to the cottages of two of her tenants, where chickenpox had broken out amongst the children. There she was kept too occupied to think of St. Clair—at least, not more than three or four times an hour.

He did fill her thoughts on the way home, however, but in a different way. Surprisingly, both of her tenants had mentioned how favourably impressed they had been by St. Clair when he had visited them.

She did not know what they meant by such remarks, nor could she fathom when or why St. Clair had visited her tenants. She was still puzzling over the matter when she went to bed that night. And she fell asleep with the thought that most certainly she would be seeing him again after all, for she thought she had a perfect right to question him on the subject.

She also fell asleep with a smile on her lips.

IN THE MORNING, she chafed at having to delay her confrontation with St. Clair, but she could not renege on her promise to Alice, and so she resigned herself to making the best of a bad lot. She would spend the day in Leeds with Alice and do her utmost to enjoy it. Tomorrow she would most definitely pay a call at Ethridge Hall.

It would have been impossible to describe the shock she felt when, stepping outside with Alice, she discovered St. Clair standing beside the carriage, talking easily with John Coachman.

He turned as they approached and said, "There you are! It is time we were leaving if we are to reach Leeds before noon."

Jane could not prevent her mouth from gaping, and he looked at her quizzically with the familiar laughter in his eyes. "What is it?" he asked. "You look as if you had seen a ghost."

"But...but..." she spluttered. "I thought you did not mean to go with us."

"Certainly I do," he replied, as though nothing out of the ordinary had occurred between them. "I thought I had made that clear several days ago."

"Yes, but..." Of course she could not complete her thoughts aloud, and was saved from thinking of another excuse for her behaviour by Alice, who was growing restive.

"Oh, do let us go!" cried the girl, and she scrambled into the carriage without waiting for assistance.

With a grin, St. Clair handed Jane in, then climbed in after her, closing the door behind them.

The carriage dipped and swayed as John Coachman climbed to the driver's seat, and a moment later the vehicle rolled forward.

For a time, they travelled along at a sedate pace, but it was not long before they gradually picked up speed and were soon bowling along at a spanking clip.

With an amused glance at Jane, St. Clair remarked, "Your coachman seems to have an inordinate fondness for speed."

Jane blushed and said, "Well, yes, but he is really an excellent driver."

"As I recall . . ." mused St. Clair.

Knowing full well that he must be remembering how their carriage had come hurtling round the bend the day they had met, Jane said quickly, "I fear John was not quite himself that day."

"You mean he was in his cups? Still, I must give him credit for being a fair marksman."

"I have apologized for that," she said crossly. "Besides, had he not been in his cups, the mishap would never have occurred."

"Oh, I would not have missed it for the world. Except for a few unpleasant aspects of the situation, I have reason to be grateful to the man. After all, I might not otherwise have met you."

She did not know how to take that, but suspected him of being sarcastic. With a swift glance at Alice, she said under her breath, "Can we not speak of this at another time?"

"By all means," he said agreeably, and for the remainder of the trip amused them with more tales of his adventures in America.

In Leeds, the day passed with amazing swiftness. The morning was taken up with poring over pattern books at the modiste's, choosing materials, and being fitted for new gowns. Jane had not intended having any made for herself, but soon convinced herself, with St. Clair's help, that it was almost a necessity. He reminded her that at some point, no doubt, she would wish to take Alice to the assemblies either here or in Harrogate, and therefore it behooved her to refurbish her own wardrobe.

She had expected that he would become quite bored with the whole, lengthy process, but he gave no indication of it. In fact, he seemed to take an extraordinary amount of interest in each step, studying patterns with them, suggesting materials, and insisting that Jane try styles which she would not, ordinarily, have chosen for herself.

His choices, of course, were of the latest fashion and far more daring than anything she was used to wearing. But Jane had to admit, when the materials were draped round her and pinned in place, they were rather becoming.

While Jane and Alice were being fitted, he sat conversing and joking with Madame Estelle. In truth, he seemed so at home in the modiste's shop that Jane couldn't decide whether to be irritated or amused by it all.

She ended by ordering far more clothes than she could comfortably afford, but she was determined not to ruin this day with thoughts of the economies she would need to practise to make up for her extravagance.

After they left Madame Estelle's, it was time to repair to the inn for the lavish nuncheon which St. Clair had ordered earlier. It proved to be so enjoyable that they lingered far longer than they should have, and Jane declared that they had only time to visit one or two more shops before heading back to Meadowbrook.

Alice protested vigorously, but Jane insisted that they did not wish to be on the road after dark. When neither adult paid the girl any heed, she soon resigned herself and they started towards the shops. They were passing a dim alley between two buildings when Jane heard an odd whimpering coming from that direction. It sounded like an injured animal, and, without a thought for the dirt or possible danger, Jane turned into the narrow space.

A short distance from the entrance, behind some discarded boxes, she discovered a small boy, curled up protectively and seemingly insensible. He was dressed in mere rags, filthy, and thin to the point of emaciation, but it was not just that which drew a shocked exclamation from her. She discovered far worse when she went down on her knees to examine him more closely.

Her companions, naturally, had followed her, and Jane looked up into St. Clair's eyes. She cried angrily, "Someone has beaten this poor child dreadfully, and ... and he looks to be covered with burns!"

"Oh, the poor thing," said Alice, peering over Jane's shoulder. "Why, he's only a baby!"

"Hardly that," said St. Clair. "He is likely older than he looks. Chimney-sweeps keep their climbing boys on the point of starvation in order to stunt their growth so they will be useful for a longer time."

He sounded so calm and matter-of-fact that Jane was about to take him to task for his lack of concern until she looked up again and noticed the grim line of his mouth.

"Is ... is he alive?" whispered Alice.

"Just barely," said Jane. "But he will not be for long if something isn't done for him soon."

"Here," said St. Clair, "let me have him. The infirmary is not far, but it is in the opposite direction. As I shall be unable to escort you back to the inn, I fear you will be obliged to accompany me."

"You could not stop me in any case!" declared Jane.

"I thought as much," answered St. Clair. Then, lifting the small, pitiful bundle, he strode out of the alley and down the street, with Jane and Alice hurrying after him, all of them ignoring the stares of passersby.

St. Clair managed everything magnificently, arranging at the infirmary for the boy to receive the best of care. But when they finally made their way back to the inn, where they had left the carriage, daylight was already waning.

Quite reasonably, St. Clair suggested that they delay their return long enough to have dinner, since it was already so late. They did, and by the time they were ready to leave, full darkness had fallen.

Just before entering the carriage, Jane apologized to John for having kept him waiting for so long.

"Oh, 'twas no trouble," he said airily, and then hiccupped loudly.

Jane could not look at St. Clair. Once they were settled in the coach, he leaned towards her and said into her ear, "I fear John Coachman is in his cups again."

"Yes," she agreed with a sigh. "But, even so, I am certain that he will get us home safely."

"*Mmm,*" murmured St. Clair.

It had been a tiring day, and they were all rather subdued. In fact, Jane's eyelids were growing heavy when she noticed that the swaying of the carriage had already lulled Alice to sleep. Seeing this as the perfect opportunity to ask St. Clair about his visits to her tenants, she sat up straighter and shook off her lethargy.

"Well, as a matter of fact, Jane," he said calmly in answer to her question, "I intended to speak to you about that as soon as we had a moment's privacy. After making a few enquiries of your tenants, I have discharged Phillips."

"Discharged!" she exclaimed, her voice rising. "What do you mean you have discharged him?"

"Keep your voice down," he said in his maddeningly calm way as he nodded towards the sleeping Alice. "I mean I have sent him packing, given him the boot. In short, I have rid you of the thieving fellow."

"Well!" said Jane, finding it difficult to express the full extent of her anger in a lowered voice. "I should like to know by what right you did such a thing! And what am I to do now, with no one to manage the estate? I tell you, St. Clair, you have gone too far!"

"Come down out of the boughs, Jane," he recommended. "My own estate manager should have no difficulty looking after Meadowbrook until I can find you a replacement."

Before she could inform him that this in no way mollified her, there came a sudden shout from outside. The carriage was pulled to a jolting halt, followed closely by the deafening explosion of a gunshot.

Alice sat up with a jerk. "What?"

"I believe this is known as *déjà vu,*" murmured St. Clair.

Thinking that he sounded entirely too nonchalant, Jane sent him a swift, disapproving look before peering out the window.

She fully expected to see a form sprawled out on the road. But, of course, even if someone were lying there, it was far too dark to see anything beyond the very limited area illuminated by the carriage lamps.

Then a deep voice cut through the darkness. "I said stand and deliver! And throw down that pistol if you don't wish to be hurt."

There came a thud as John hastened to be accommodating, and then someone moved into the light. A rather large someone, cloaked in black, seated atop a huge black horse and pointing his own pistol towards John and the carriage.

This, most certainly, was the highwayman Jane had all but put from her mind once she discovered St. Clair's true identity. They were about to be robbed by him, unless St. Clair— Oh dear, she hoped he would not attempt something foolish....

CHAPTER THIRTEEN

WELL, THAT HAD BEEN another needless worry, Jane found herself thinking as St. Clair handed her down from the carriage a few moments later. One would have thought from his behaviour that being robbed at gunpoint by a highwayman was an everyday occurrence. She didn't know why she felt so vexed when he was merely fulfilling her hope that he would not play the hero. Of course she was glad of that, but on the other hand, he needn't have taken everything so casually, either.

When they were all on the ground, the highwayman said, "Now, sir, if you will be so good as to hand me the ladies' reticules and jewels, and your own purse, too...."

St. Clair took one step forward, and Alice moved nearer to Jane, so that they were both standing close together behind him. He glanced back at them but made no move to take the reticules they held out to him. Instead, he turned back to the highwayman and said calmly, "I think not."

Jane's heart leapt into her throat and, on the instant, she bitterly regretted any wish she had entertained that he might not prove to be cowardly.

The highwayman seemed to have been taken aback, for he remained silent for several moments. But then he waved his pistol slightly and said, sounding rather desperate, "I don't wish to harm anyone, but I shall if you don't do as I say."

"That would be quite unwise, my friend," said St. Clair. "At this very moment, there is another pistol pointed at the back of your head."

The highwayman gave a rather forced-sounding laugh. "A good trick, if I were fool enough to be taken in by it, but I'm not. Now, hand over your valuables and be done with it."

St. Clair sighed and said, "Kearny?"

Several things happened in rapid succession. Another explosion filled the air; the highwayman dropped his pistol and clutched his right shoulder with his left hand; the black horse danced with fright; and, losing his balance, the highwayman fell to the ground. He landed with a loud thud and a moan, then fell silent and lay quite still.

For a moment, no one moved or said anything. Jane, feeling rather dazed, thought that, except for a few minor details, the whole thing seemed uncannily like a reenactment of her meeting with St. Clair. She almost expected to see him lying there, bleeding on the ground, and shuddered at the thought.

She was brought back to reality as St. Clair said casually, "My dear man, you might have merely fired a warning shot over his head."

Kearny guided his horse into view, saying, "No sense takin' chances. Not with ladies here an' all."

Scarcely hearing them, Jane said, "I believe the poor man has hit his head and knocked himself senseless." With that, she brushed past St. Clair and hurried towards the man on the ground.

"Here now, ma'am!" Kearny exclaimed. "You shouldn't ought to do that. Leastways, not till one of us takes a look-see. He could just be playin' possum."

Jane threw him a puzzled glance but did not stop.

Sounding highly amused, St Clair said, "You are wasting your breath, Kearny. I doubt you could stop her even with that pistol. The lady is irresistibly attracted to the wounded. But if it will make you feel better, I do not think our friend capable of harming her. He no longer has his weapon, and judging from the sound his head made when it hit the ground, he is likely to be unconscious for a good length of time."

Kearny shook his head, and gazed at St. Clair with wonder. "In all this time, I ain't never got used to the way you talk."

Jane rolled her eyes at that, but by now she was on her knees beside the wounded man and all her attention became fixed on determining how badly he was injured. Without being told, John Coachman had brought one of the carriage lanterns to give her better light.

Alice, peering over Jane's shoulder, suddenly giggled and said, "So this is Papa's 'devilish rogue.' He doesn't look so devilish or roguish to me. In fact, he looks rather nice."

Until then, Jane had been concentrating on the man's wounded arm, but now she looked up. With his hat no longer hiding his hair or face, she saw that he was fairly young, blond, and fair of skin. And, indeed, he did not look in the least like a villain. St. Clair looked far more dangerous.

"Fortunately, he appears to have no more than a flesh wound," she said. "Of course, it must still be cleansed and bandaged, but I am more worried about a possible head injury." She paused, biting her lip. "I wish I had my basket of medicaments with me! But, as I have not, there is only one thing to be done. We must get him into the carriage and take him to Meadowbrook with us."

"Oh, no! You shall not," St. Clair informed her quite firmly.

Suddenly reminded that they were not dealing with a respectable man, Jane realized that St Clair would be planning to turn him over to the authorities.

Looking up at him in dismay, she exclaimed, "Oh, but, Jon, only look at him! Indeed, he does not look like a criminal. You cannot have him arrested without giving him a chance to explain."

In her distress, she was unaware how she had addressed him. She only knew that his expression unaccountably softened.

With a slight smile he said, "No, I have not made up my mind as to that, but in the meantime, he shall stay at Ethridge Hall, not at Meadowbrook. I shall not have you wearing yourself to a thread and further damaging your reputation by caring for another wounded man in your home. And *this* one not even a cousin.''

''But—'' she began.

''No, don't argue,'' he interrupted her. ''I have servants at the Hall who will see that he receives care. And you may visit him as often as you wish, as his physician. I see no harm in that, since *his* wound is in a perfectly innocuous spot.''

''Jon!'' she exclaimed in an undertone.

Glancing round, and finding that the others had moved sufficiently far away, he murmured, ''Do you know, I have never cared for that name before, but I like hearing it upon your lips.''

Fortunately, the darkness helped to hide her fiery blush. At least she hoped it did. In an attempt to hide her discomposure, she stood, brushed her skirts and said briskly, ''Well, we must not stand about like this all night. John, if you and Mr. Kearny will be so good as to lift our patient into the carriage, we may be on our way.''

She could not bring herself to look at St. Clair again but was certain that if she did, she would discover the familiar laughter there. He was truly incorrigible, she thought, and her own lips twitched slightly.

But then she frowned as she was struck by the thought that she was allowing herself to fall ever more deeply in love with him when she ought to know better. Flirtation, she knew, came as naturally to him as breathing. She must accept that and be grateful he was still her friend. To allow herself to begin hoping for more would be foolish beyond permission.

When they were all settled in the carriage, the exertions and stresses of the day began to make themselves felt, and no one seemed inclined to speak. But after a time, Jane roused herself enough to say, "I suppose it was very fortunate for us that Mr. Kearny turned up as he did."

St. Clair laughed. "Good fortune had nothing to do with it. I knew he would be close by. I once made the mistake of doing the fellow a good turn and now I cannot rid myself of him. Not that he doesn't have his uses. In fact, I have grown almost fond of him."

Alice giggled. "A good turn! I'll wager you saved his life."

St. Clair shrugged. "It is a long story, and boring, to boot."

As he seemed disinclined to enlarge upon the subject, neither of his companions questioned him further.

The remainder of their journey was accomplished in relative silence. And, despite her best intentions, both medical and otherwise, by the time they reached Meadowbrook, Jane was utterly exhausted—so exhausted, in fact, that she could scarcely think, let alone remember good intentions. She accepted without demur, therefore, St. Clair's opinion that it was unnecessary for her to make the trip to Ethridge Hall that night. He assured her that he himself would cleanse the man's wound, disinfect it according to her directions, and bandage it.

But, in spite of her weariness, when he handed her down from the carriage and did not immediately release her hand, she stood gazing at him idiotishly. She even felt herself swaying towards him until he finally freed her hand, and clearing his throat, said, "Well, I shall wish you a good night, my dear."

She nodded and followed Alice into the house, knowing that she had come near to making a cake of herself once more, but too tired to care. It did seem to her that he had been equally disinclined to part, but very likely that was merely wishful thinking. Exhaustion could do peculiar things to one's mind.

JANE BECAME even more convinced that she had imagined his reluctance to leave her when she arrived at Ethridge Hall the following morning. St. Clair greeted her in quite his usual manner, friendly but casual, before taking her upstairs to see her patient.

The young man, whose name, she learned, was George Davies, was awake. Though he was a trifle pale and admitted to a slight headache, he seemed not to be suffering from concussion. Jane soon discovered, however, that he was exceedingly shy.

While it was refreshing to meet someone who blushed more easily than she had been doing of late, his diffidence made conversation uphill work. After a few unsuccessful attempts at drawing him out, Jane gave up and took refuge in her role as physician.

There, too, she was quickly brought to a standstill. St. Clair had done an excellent job of caring for the wound, so that all that was left for her to do was to apply a fresh bandage to it and advise Mr. Davies to rest. After which, she made a hasty retreat.

The whole had taken barely a quarter of an hour. Jane was more than a little disappointed, for without a patient needing her care, she would have no further excuse for visiting Ethridge Hall. However, today at least, she had reason to linger. There were still one or two matters she needed to discuss with St. Clair.

She was halfway down the staircase and wondering where he might be, when he stepped out of a room on the far side of the entry hall below.

With his eyes laughing up at her, he said, "I thought it would not be long. How did you find your patient?"

"Well," she answered cautiously, "he *seems* quite fit, but one can never be sure about these things."

"Oh, I agree," he said solemnly. "With injuries such as his, one can never be too careful."

She looked at him sharply, strongly suspecting that he was teasing her, but she merely nodded and continued down the stairs.

When she reached the bottom, he said, "Come into the library. I wish to talk with you about the business of Meadowbrook. I feel I owe you a more detailed explanation regarding my discharging of Phillips."

"As do I," she told him, sweeping through the double doors.

She noticed that he carefully left the doors ajar when he followed her in, but by then, it had come to her for the first time that she was actually inside Ethridge Hall.

Standing in the middle of the huge, rectangular room, she slowly turned round, taking in all the details. It did not disappoint her. It was everything she had imagined, and more.

Opposite the doors was an enormous fireplace over which hung a large oil painting of a country scene. Both fireplace and doors were flanked by more paintings and shelves of books. Books lined a third wall as well, and in the fourth, floor-to-ceiling windows let in abundant daylight. Two exquisite chandeliers and several candelabra ensured that the room would always be well lit. A beautiful Aubusson carpet covered nearly the whole expanse of the floor. Scattered about the delightful room were groupings of sofas, chairs and small tables.

With a sigh, Jane at last turned to St. Clair and said, "Oh, it is perfect! If you knew how often I have fantasized about this house..." She stopped, feeling the heat of a blush rising in her cheeks again.

But St. Clair seemed pleased. "I am very glad that you approve. It is my favourite room, and in fact, the first I had done, after the bedchambers and kitchens. I shan't give you a tour, however, until the entire place is finished, for I shouldn't wish you to be disappointed."

"I doubt I should be," she replied with a smile. "Nevertheless, I shall wait."

He then gestured towards one of the seating areas. She sat down at one end of a sofa, while St. Clair chose a chair set at right angles to it.

"Before we get into the matter of Meadowbrook," Jane said quickly, "I should like to thank you."

He raised his eyebrows. "For what?"

"For not turning the highwayman over to the authorities immediately."

He grinned. "How could I show less compassion than you? After all, you did not cry rope on me when you thought me to be the culprit."

"Yes, well..." she muttered, and, of course, she blushed.

"To be perfectly truthful," he said more seriously, "I had another reason for not turning him in."

"Oh?"

"Yes, rampant curiosity," he admitted with another grin. "Not only did the fellow look to be the least likely in the world to be a criminal, but his speech indicated a certain amount of breeding and education."

"Yes, I noticed that, too," she said eagerly. "What do you make of it?"

"Well, to begin with, I thought it probable that his story was similar to the one you attributed to me when you thought I was the highwayman. And, in fact, I have learned since that at least a portion of it is."

"Do you mean to say that he has actually talked to you? I could scarcely get a word out of him."

"He *is* a trifle shy—which, again, is not what one would expect of a highwayman—but perhaps that condition is more apparent in the company of females."

"Most likely," she agreed, already beginning to fashion a history for Mr. Davies. "He seems very young, and perhaps his mother died at an early age, and he had no sisters, so is unused to..."

She stopped when she noticed a slow, knowing smile beginning to form on St. Clair's lips, and said quickly, "But what did he tell you?"

"It seems that our highwayman, whom I think we should begin referring to as Mr. Davies, was born on the wrong side of the blanket. His father was a member of the gentry and quite wealthy, and to his credit, he acknowledged the boy, rearing him on his estate and having him educated along with his other children.

"Unfortunately, the other children were not so inclined to accept Mr. Davies, and when the father stuck his spoon in the wall, the heir gave our hero the boot. Mr. Davies then enlisted in the army and managed to survive to the end of the war. It is the remainder of the story which you will find familiar.

"Upon returning to England, he could not find gainful employment, and being a resourceful young man, he turned to the life of a highwayman."

"Well," said Jane, "as you once said, I am sure he preferred that to begging. In any event, I do not think we should turn him in."

"No," St. Clair agreed. "As a matter of fact, I believe I may have a much better solution for him."

"Oh? What is that?"

But he smiled and shook his head, saying, "It is early days yet to speak of it. I shall need more information from Mr. Davies before I make a decision. And, of course, he must agree to the plan, too."

"Very well," said Jane. "I shall leave the problem of Mr. Davies to you, so long as I need not worry about him being hanged." She paused and caught her lower lip between her teeth. "And since he is doing so well, I suppose I need not worry about him in a medical sense, either, which means it will not be necessary for me to look in on him every day."

"How can you say so?" he asked. "It is quite possible that he may exhibit delayed symptoms of concussion. I have known such things to happen—in the army, you know."

"Of course!" said Jane. "I had not thought of that. Well, then," she added cheerfully, rising, "I shall see you again in the morning, if I am not needed sooner."

"Oh, but you cannot leave yet," he told her. "My chef has gone to a great deal of trouble preparing us an excellent nuncheon. And you know how I hate to eat alone."

It did not take much to persuade her, for of course, she did not wish to offend St. Clair's chef. And the repast was indeed excellent. Jane enjoyed it very much, but she enjoyed St. Clair's company even more.

They spoke of all manner of things, from poor Beau Brummell's flight from England to escape his creditors, to the odd Sioux custom of rubbing noses rather than kissing, which he had observed in America.

"However," St. Clair informed her, "when I left, many of them had already accepted our custom in preference to theirs, and with great enthusiasm, I might add."

Having drunk two glasses of wine with the meal, Jane shook her head at him and said with mock severity, "You are attempting to put me to the blush again, St. Clair."

"How did you guess?" he asked with laughing eyes.

"Very easily," she retorted. "I am beginning to know you quite well, you see."

It was, perhaps, fortunate that, in the process of rising from the table, she did not notice the look he gave her.

As they moved towards the door together, she said, "I have enjoyed this very much, but now I really must go. Poor Agatha will think I have run away."

"I doubt poor Agatha will worry overmuch," he murmured, with just a touch of sarcasm. But she was several steps ahead of him, and when she asked him to repeat his words, he said blandly, "I doubt that Agatha will worry. After all, she knows where you are."

"Yes, but I have stayed much longer than I meant to do. Sir Alfred called just before I left, and I fear that he and Agatha may come to blows if they are left alone too long. So, dear sir, I shall bid you farewell, until tomorrow."

He did not attempt to dissuade her again, and Jane was soon riding home, filled with a remarkable sense of well-being. She was almost at her doorstep before she remembered that they had never got round to discussing Meadowbrook or Phillips.

But, after a moment, she shrugged that concern away. There was always tomorrow, she thought, and stepped lightly into the house.

CHAPTER FOURTEEN

THE NEXT MORNING, after a brief visit with her patient, Jane and St. Clair finally got round to discussing Meadowbrook and Phillips.

Jane was shocked and chagrined when she learned how Phillips had been cheating her for the past four years. But there could be no mistaking the matter. St. Clair showed her the vast difference between the account books kept while her father still lived and those after his death. And he explained just how the man had done it.

"I feel like such a ninny," she said with a great deal of self-disgust. "I have always prided myself on my intelligence, but not to have seen what was happening!"

"How should you have seen it?" St. Clair asked. "Phillips is a very clever man—I'll grant him that much. And, from all that I have heard about your father, I doubt that you received any training in estate management."

"No," she admitted. "What little I do know, I taught myself. But I see now that there is a great deal more to it than I thought."

"Indeed," said St. Clair.

"Well," said Jane, "I shall simply have to learn more about the matter. I do not wish to impose, but would you help me? Perhaps you could lend me some books on the subject."

"Gladly, but I shall do better than that," he replied. "It is always good for an owner to be knowledgeable, but what you really need is another bailiff. This time, one who is both reliable and honest."

"Yes," agreed Jane slowly. She caught her lower lip in her teeth, wondering how she was going to accomplish that.

"I shall take care of it," said St. Clair.

She immediately bristled. "I am perfectly capable of solving my own problems, St. Clair. I have been independent for four years."

"I've no doubt of it," he replied. "And I admire you tremendously, I promise you. But at the moment your plate is full, what with managing your household, caring for the ill of the district, and attempting to bring Alice up to snuff. Why should you go to the trouble when I am perfectly willing to do it for you? You must allow me to do this service for you as your... friend."

"Well, when you put it that way..." said Jane. She wondered why his affirmation of their friendship should leave her feeling less than happy.

"Good girl!" he said, then added, "As a matter of fact, I already have someone in mind for the position."

"Oh? Who?"

"I'd rather not say just now, in case it does not work out. But it does look very promising."

"Very well," said Jane. "I shall leave the matter to you."

She strongly suspected what he had in mind, but decided to pretend ignorance and allow him to go about this in his own way. And, when he told her that Mr. Davies was his candidate for the job, she would act surprised and pleased. She had some trouble suppressing a smile, for the incongruity of the terms "reliable and honest" as applied to a retired highwayman did not escape her.

True to his word, St. Clair supplied Jane with several weighty tomes from his library, then laughed at her look of dismay. Fortunately, she was not required to wade through them at once, for he proposed to spend the succeeding days riding with her over both her land and his own in order to teach her the basics of estate management.

They began her instruction that same day. Even so tedious a business proved to be enjoyable, for St. Clair made it interesting by telling humorous anecdotes and fascinating bits of agricultural history.

"How is it that you know so much about all this?" she asked at one point. "I would not have thought a man such as you..." She stopped, realizing that she might be insulting him.

But he merely laughed. "You mean a rake such as I? As a matter of fact, I surprise myself, but I suppose I must have absorbed more than I knew while growing up here."

It was late afternoon when St. Clair called a halt to the day's lesson. Jane was surprised at how quickly the hours had flown. She had so enjoyed herself that she hated to part from him, and she was delighted when he insisted upon escorting her back to Meadowbrook. She was even more pleased when he accepted her invitation to come in for tea.

They entered the house to hear a familiar booming voice. "If that ain't exactly like a female! It just goes to show that you know nothing about the matter."

Jane and St. Clair stopped in the drawing-room doorway as Agatha retorted, "I know that your fat friend will be the ruination of this country if he continues with his extravagance and his dissipated ways!"

"Fat friend!" cried Sir Alfred, clearly outraged. "Now you have gone too far, woman. 'Twas those very words helped put the finishing touch to Brummell's downfall."

"Oh, good heavens, they are at it again," murmured Jane, and she hurried into the room.

Catching sight of her, Sir Alfred beamed and said, "Ah, there you are, my dear. A sight for sore eyes, I must say."

He was struggling to rise from his place on the sofa and, although his foot was less heavily bandaged today, Jane made haste to stop him. "Pray, do not try to get up, Sir Alfred. I know your gout must be paining you, so I shall excuse you from such gallantry."

He sank back with obvious relief, but assured her, "Oh, the blasted thing is much better. Agatha has been using one of your miracle cures on me."

He beamed at Jane again, then gestured towards St. Clair. "Glad to see you, my boy. Come here and see if you can set this hen-witted woman straight."

Sauntering further into the room, St. Clair rested one arm along the mantle. "Now how am I to answer that, sir? In truth, I see no hen-witted woman here."

"Oh, very well. I shall own that Agatha ain't pea-brained, but she has some damned queer notions in that head of hers."

"If you wish to stay for tea, Alfred," warned Agatha, "you will watch your language."

"Now what did I say?" he demanded.

Hoping to avert another quarrel between them, Jane asked, "What is it that you think Agatha does not understand, Sir Alfred?"

"She don't understand that Prinny's memorial to the Stuarts won't cost the government a cent. You tell her, St. Clair."

"Actually, he is right," St. Clair admitted ruefully. "France will be paying for it."

"Perhaps," said Agatha doubtfully as she scowled at Sir Alfred. "But what about his endless renovations to Carlton House and that monstrosity in Brighton? You will not tell me *those* are not draining the treasury!"

Fortunately, Melrose entered the room just then with the tea tray.

Sir Alfred patted the place beside him on the sofa and said to Jane, "Come here and tell me what you have been up to, my dear. Agatha will pour for us."

Jane missed St. Clair's slight frown as she obligingly sat down next to the squire. Rather than telling him about her day, however, she looked round and asked, "Where is Alice?"

"Oh," said Agatha, "she is spending the day with her friend Clarissa. I thought the break would do her no harm."

Jane merely nodded, momentarily wondering if she should feel guilty for neglecting the girl when in fact she did not.

The conversation then turned to less controversial topics. A short time later Melrose again entered the room to say, "Pardon me, Miss Jane, but a message has just arrived for Lord St. Clair."

Frowning again, St. Clair crossed the room and took the slip of paper from the butler.

"I hope it is not bad news," said Jane.

"No, but I fear I must take my leave of you. It seems that I have acquired some unexpected guests."

Jane did not know what to make of his expression. She could not decide if the look in his eyes was one of anger or excitement.

She walked with him to the door, and they waited on the steps for his horse to be brought round. He seemed preoccupied. She supposed that his mind was on his visitors. She wondered who they might be, but he did not offer to tell her, and she could not bring herself to ask.

She was completely taken aback when he suddenly turned to her and demanded, "Is that damned fellow here every day?"

She blinked. "Who?"

"Sir Alfred."

"Of course not. Besides, it has been but a few days since his return from Brighton."

"And I'll wager he has spent most of that time at Meadowbrook. Does he take his meals with you, too?"

"Well, sometimes," she admitted, wondering what on earth all this was about. "But you must remember that it cannot be very comfortable at the Manor with so many of his servants away."

"I saw how he fawned over you today. The man is dangling after you, Jane, and I do not think it wise to encourage him."

Jane gaped at him before bursting into laughter. "Good God, St Clair! How can you be so absurd? That is just his way. In any case, if he is dangling after anyone, it is Agatha."

"Now who is talking nonsense? You know as well as I that the two of them rub along together like a cat and a dog."

"Yes," she agreed, looking thoughtful, "but do you know, I am beginning to believe that they actually enjoy their bickering."

Jackson appeared then with St. Clair's horse, so their conversation was brought to a close. St. Clair swung into the saddle and said tersely, "I shall see you tomorrow."

Jane watched him as he urged Achilles into a canter and disappeared down the drive. She wished their parting had been a trifle more amicable. Now that he had friends at the Hall, she doubted that he would have time to spend tutoring her. Nevertheless, he obviously expected her to continue her calls on her patient, and she breathed a sigh of relief.

As HE RODE towards the Hall, St. Clair's mood was far from amiable. As if he did not have enough problems, what with Lydia finally chasing him down—and apparently bringing a houseful of company with her—now he must worry about that old reprobate making up to Jane.

Jane might say what she liked, but he had seen the way Sir Alfred looked at her, and God help him, St. Clair was fully aware of just how desirable she was. He only hoped that he had given her food for thought so that she would not unwittingly lead the old squire on.

As he drew nearer to Ethridge Hall and the woman awaiting him there, another thought struck him. What would happen when Jane and Lydia met?

He gritted his teeth, cursed under his breath and rode on.

CHAPTER FIFTEEN

IT WAS with some trepidation that Jane called at Ethridge Hall the next morning to see Mr. Davies. Despite St. Clair's parting words, she had begun to feel that she was on shaky ground with these casual visits to his home. She was well aware that some people might view them as improper.

In addition, although she was still curious about St. Clair's guests, she had decided that they must all be very witty, worldly, interesting, and stylish. In short, all the things she was not. It had also occurred to her that, since he was such a notorious rake, his friends might not move in the first circles of Society. Whatever the case, she feared that he would see her in a less favourable light by comparison.

The house seemed remarkably quiet when she was admitted by the butler and shown up to Mr. Davies's chamber. She wondered at this until she recalled that members of the fashionable world did not seek their beds till dawn and seldom rose before noon. Even St. Clair, who was usually there to greet her, was nowhere about, and she could only assume that he had reverted to London hours.

She tried to ignore her disappointment as she fussed over Mr. Davies, changing his dressing and seeing to his comfort. Her patient still displayed a strong tendency towards blushing, but he was gradually becoming less reserved in her presence, which made it easier to prolong her visit with him. Even so, it was far short of noon when she made her way back downstairs, and she was resigned to the unlikelihood of seeing St. Clair or his friends today. It therefore came as a most agreeable surprise to find him awaiting her in the entry hall.

Doing her best to hide her pleasure at the sight of him, she said, "Good morning, St. Clair. I have just come from seeing Mr. Davies."

"And how did you find him this morning?"

"Very well," she told him. "He is even beginning to lose some of his shyness with me."

St. Clair merely smiled, and taking her arm, asked, "Shall we go?"

"Go?" she repeated blankly.

He cocked a brow at her. "Have you forgotten our project? I was to acquaint you with the basics of estate management, was I not?"

"Yes, but I shall not hold you to that now that you have guests to entertain."

"Oh, I think I can spare you an hour or two. Besides, I feel no obligation to provide them with entertainment, since they came without invitation."

Jane was not going to argue with him. She was too delighted to discover that her lessons were not to be discontinued after all.

They rode for a time without speaking, but it was not the easy, companionable silence they had sometimes shared. In fact, he seemed so preoccupied that she finally said, "A penny for your thoughts, St. Clair."

Smiling ruefully, he answered, "I fear they are not worth even so much as that."

After a brief hesitation she asked, "Do they concern your friends?"

A slight frown appeared on his brow. "I believe it would be more accurate to describe them as acquaintances."

Jane did not know what to make of that but, since she did not wish to display a vulgar curiosity by questioning him further, she said nothing.

For a time, St. Clair, too, refrained from speaking. Then he suddenly pulled Achilles to a halt and turned towards her.

Jane drew up beside him and looked at him enquiringly.

"Jane," he began, "about these guests of mine..."

"Yes?"

He ran his fingers through his hair. "Actually, what I wish to tell you concerns one of them in particular. She—" He stopped abruptly, and they both turned at the sound of a rapidly approaching horse.

Jane thought she heard him mutter, "Damnation," under his breath, but she was too stunned by what she saw to heed his reaction.

The rider of the horse was a female. An extremely beautiful female, with red-gold hair, vivid green eyes, and a flawless complexion. Her figure, too, was superb, and it was shown off to great advantage by her modish riding habit. To make matters worse, she was petite. Looking at her, Jane suddenly felt like a homely giantess.

This piece of perfection reined in beside Achilles and said playfully, "For shame, St. Clair! One would almost think you were attempting to avoid me."

"I hardly expected you to be up and about so early, Lydia," he replied.

"Usually I am not, but I find it quite difficult to sleep when in the country. The appalling quiet keeps waking me."

He gave a short laugh. "Perhaps I should hire a hackney coach to drive to and fro beneath your window as Alvanley once did for a friend with the same complaint."

"Oh, what a delightful notion! Yes, I think you should do that for me, St. Clair."

Suddenly seeming to recall his manners, St. Clair said, "Lydia, you must allow me to introduce you to my neighbor, Jane Lockwood. Jane, this is Lady Cathcart."

"How do you do, my lady," Jane said politely.

After quickly taking in Jane's appearance from head to toe, Lady Cathcart offered her a condescending smile. "Do call me Lydia," she said. Then, glancing from St. Clair to Jane, she added, "I hope you will not mind if I join you for your ride."

"As a matter of fact..." began St. Clair.

At the same time, Jane exclaimed, "Oh, I was merely consulting with St. Clair on a matter to do with my own estate, but as we are finished, I really must be going. It was lovely meeting you...Lydia. And thank you for your advice, St. Clair."

Having already turned her horse before the last words left her mouth, Jane rode away as quickly as she could without giving the impression of undue haste.

From the first, she had known that her love for St. Clair was hopeless, but now that truth had been brought home to her more forcefully than ever. And it was surprisingly painful, given that she thought she had relinquished all expectations save those of friendship. Well, apparently she had been wrong. Obviously she had still been entertaining impossible dreams, but she could no longer delude herself. What man in his right mind would choose plain Jane Lockwood over the beautiful Lydia Cathcart?

She arrived at Meadowbrook in a state of despondency which she did her best to hide upon entering the house. There she discovered Sir Alfred in the midst of another argument with Agatha.

The two broke off their dispute to greet Jane, and Agatha demanded, "Well? Did you discover who St. Clair's guests are?"

Jane sat down before answering, "No, but I did meet one of them—a Lady Cathcart."

"Ah," said Sir Alfred knowingly. "Heard she was after him, which goes to prove I was right. A man can be forgiven anything if he has enough blunt."

"Who is she, Alfred?" asked Agatha.

"Old Algernon's widow. Married the earl when he was at his last prayers and did very well for herself."

Agatha sniffed. "I suppose she is no better than she should be."

"No, no," he assured her. "A trifle fast, but very good ton for all that. No, 'tis marriage she's after, though there's no saying but what she might settle for less if she fails to bring him up to the mark."

Jane stood abruptly and asked in a slightly strangled voice, "Where is Alice?"

"She is in the garden, practising her water-colours," said Agatha.

Jane was already halfway across the room as she told them, "I believe I shall go and see how she is coming along."

Agatha merely nodded before saying, "Now tell me this, Alfred ..."

Thankfully, Jane heard no more. She longed for a period of solitude in order to untangle her chaotic thoughts but, knowing that she had been neglecting Alice of late, she dutifully made her way to the garden. She spent what remained of the morning with the girl, and it was not until early afternoon that she was able to find time for herself.

She had scarcely entered her chamber, however, when Melrose came to say that Lord St. Clair was below, asking for her. Her first impulse was to deny herself to him but she quickly decided against that. She must face him sooner or later and she doubted that postponement would make their meeting any easier. Her best course of action would be to treat him in the same friendly manner as always, no matter how difficult that might be.

In fact, it proved to be easier than she had expected. "St. Clair," she said upon reaching the entry hall. "This is a surprise. I did not think to see you again today."

Taking both her hands in his, he replied, "No, but I contrived to send everyone off to Leeds for the remainder of the day, so we may take up where we left off this morning."

She hesitated but could think of no excuse that he would not easily counter. Besides, unwise though it was, she wanted to be with him. She finally said, "Very well. I shall only be a few minutes," and she hurried upstairs to change back into her riding habit.

They ended the afternoon on the very spot where they had held their picnic. And if, when he lifted her down from her saddle, he left his hands on her waist a trifle longer than necessary, it was not long enough for her to take exception to. Not that she would have done so in any case, she admitted to herself.

To banish that thought, she said brightly, "Oh, what a perfect ending, St. Clair. You remembered that this is one of my favourite places."

He merely smiled as he removed his coat and spread it on the ground for her to sit on. And, though Jane made a token protest, she accepted without comment his avowal that it was an old garment which would not be harmed.

He sat down beside her then, and Jane scarcely noticed the silence which fell between them, for she was hearing her own words of a few minutes earlier repeated in her mind.

When she had spoken, she had meant that it was a perfect way to end the day, but she knew that more than just their day together was ending. That would be true even if Lady Cathcart had not arrived on the scene.

St. Clair had taught her all that it was necessary for her to know, and she could no longer use Mr. Davies as an excuse for visiting the Hall. His mind was as clear as a bell, and he had not complained of the headache since that first day. Even she could not continue pretending that his wound was anything other than a scratch.

Moreover, St. Clair had discovered that, having been reared on his father's estate, Mr. Davies knew a great deal about estate management. So, when the position at Meadowbrook was offered to him, he had accepted with alacrity and gratitude. There was no further excuse for Jane to seek St. Clair's company. Besides, she had been neglecting her own chores at Meadowbrook quite deplorably, and really should get back to them.

Knowing that now was the time to stop procrastinating, she licked her suddenly dry lips, turned her head to look at him, and said, "St. Clair—"

She stopped abruptly when she discovered him staring at her lips intently. Her heart suddenly seemed to be beating quite erratically.

Before she could even think, he grasped her shoulders, pulled her hard against his chest, and brought his mouth down on hers almost angrily. But, in the next instant, the hint of anger disappeared, and his kisses became all that she remembered them to be.

Gently his mouth moved over hers, shaping and moulding. Then his tongue came seeking, and with her welcoming co-operation, plunged into her mouth, exploring, teasing, inviting, until she finally followed his lead. Tentatively at first, and then more daringly, she allowed her tongue to learn the sweet taste of his mouth.

It was heavenly, but it was not enough. She longed, as she had before, to feel his hand on her breast, and instinctively she pressed herself closer against his chest. He made a sound deep in his throat, and when one of his hands left her shoulder to move downward, she was filled with a sense of fierce joy, breathless expectation, and all manner of wildly wonderful sensations. Once again she was completely unprepared when he abruptly pulled away and, with a muffled oath, turned from her.

Blessedly, for a moment at least, her mind was numb, but not so numb that she did not hear him mutter, "Damnation!"

She waited for him to continue, feeling as if her whole fate hung in the balance, but he did not continue.

Instead, he gave a harsh laugh, and said with mocking formality, "Well, it seems I must beg your forgiveness once again, Miss Lockwood. My only excuse is that I must have spent too long rusticating away from London."

Jane could not mistake his meaning, nor could she answer him. She was too busy berating herself, attempting to swallow the lump in her throat, and fighting the tears in her eyes.

And something else, which she could not yet identify, was trying to push its way up through all her misery.

He spoke again, and this time his voice sounded gentle and apologetic. And worse—far worse—she could detect a note of pity in it. He said, "I fear I would make a most unsuitable husband, Jane. More to the point, marriage has never interested me, and you, I know, would settle for nothing less."

And now Jane could identify what that something else was. It was anger. At herself, certainly, but this time the anger extended to him, too. She had behaved brazenly but he was not blameless. She might have unwittingly instigated that first incident, but he had, without doubt, begun this one. And now, he had added insult to injury.

Before he could stop her—if he had even wished to, which she doubted—Jane jumped to her feet, strode to her horse, and pulled herself into the saddle.

Coldly, she said, "If you will excuse me, Lord St. Clair, I really must be going now."

As she flicked the reins, he called, "Jane, wait!"

Despite herself, she stopped, but she did not turn to face him and her back remained ramrod straight.

After a moment, she heard him sigh heavily before saying, "I shall be returning to London tomorrow."

"Have a pleasant journey," she said coolly, and urged her horse forward.

For some time, as she rode home to Meadow-brook, Jane was uplifted by her anger, as well as pride in the way she had conducted herself at the last. She had neither wept, pleaded, nor berated, all of which she had, by turns, felt like doing. Instead, she had remained calm, cool, and civil, just as a lady ought.

And she *was* a lady, despite the fact that too often of late she had failed to behave like one. But she was no longer bewitched by St. Clair. All that was over. Ended.

It was too bad that anger and pride did not continue to sustain her. Unfortunately, both deserted her long before Meadowbrook came into view. No sooner had she thought of endings than the full extent of her loss bore down upon her, and she was filled with pain and grief. And telling herself that she was better off without him could not ease the ache in her chest or help to hold back her tears.

By the time she reached Meadowbrook, she had composed herself sufficiently to face Melrose. But she feared she would lose her precarious control at the least sign of sympathy, which Agatha was sure to administer in abundance.

For that reason, she was grateful to discover that Agatha and Alice were from home. And even more so when Melrose informed her that they would be returning late, as they intended to dine with Sir Alfred.

She spent the next few hours in her chamber, weeping, wishing, praying. But she knew that it was useless to hope. It was over. She would never see him again, and if she did, they would meet as polite acquaintances. With that thought, the cycle started all over again.

She wondered how it was humanly possible to bear such pain, but knew that she must. There was no other choice. One did not, after all, die of a broken heart.

CHAPTER SIXTEEN

BY THE TIME Agatha and Alice returned, Jane had composed herself once more. She had come to the conclusion that she was not going to die, and must, therefore, live with the pain of St. Clair's loss. And although inside she might feel as if she were dying, a lady did not show her emotions.

Besides, it would be unfair to subject others to her misery. There was nothing so tedious, she knew, as being forced to endure the company of one who was forever sunk in gloom. The best thing she could do, for herself and those around her, would be to act as normally as possible, and also to keep herself too busy to wallow in her unhappiness.

And so, when Agatha and Alice finally returned, she was awaiting them in the drawing-room, and was able to greet them pleasantly, if not quite cheerfully.

"What have you two been up to?" she asked. "I am afraid I have been neglecting you quite dreadfully, but all that is in the past. I intend to remain at home now and attend to my duties."

"Oh," said Agatha, "we have been going along very well on our own, I promise you. So there is no need for you to desert Mr. Davies and Lord St. Clair."

"Well, as to that," said Jane, fighting to keep her voice steady, "Mr. Davies is quite fit now. As a matter of fact, he is to be our new estate agent."

"Oh," said Agatha again. "But what a marvellous solution to our problems! You know, I could not quite like imposing upon St. Clair's man, and this is so much better than having poor Mr. Davies hanged."

Alice giggled at that, and Jane was even able to smile a little as she agreed. Then she added, in what she hoped was a casual manner, "As for St. Clair, I believe he means to return to London tomorrow."

"Whatever for?" asked Agatha, clearly astonished. "London is completely dead at this time of year. No one of any consequence will be there."

"I doubt he cares for that," Jane replied, unable to keep a touch of bitterness from her voice, since she was quite certain that Lady Cathcart would accompany him. She could not resist adding, "I am certain that there will always be some attractions there for a man such as he."

Agatha frowned at that, and turning to Alice, said, "I believe, my dear, that it is past time for you to retire."

To Jane's amazement, Alice did not argue, although her countenance took on a pouting expression. After wishing them a slightly ungracious goodnight, the girl took herself off to bed.

"My goodness!" exclaimed Jane. "How did you manage that?"

"I am not completely useless as a mentor, my dear Jane," Agatha informed her. "If you will recall, I was your governess before I became your companion."

"Of course," said Jane in a much chastened voice. "It is just that I am so used to thinking of you as my friend, it is difficult to remember you as an authority figure."

"Humph," said Agatha. "But to return to the subject of St. Clair, how long does he plan to remain in London?"

"I haven't the least notion," replied Jane.

"But he does mean to return to Ethridge Hall, does he not?"

"I don't believe so."

"Oh, Jane, you did not have a falling out with him, did you?"

"Of course not. Whatever put such a ridiculous idea into your head?"

"But I thought he meant to remain here indefinitely. I thought... I thought..."

"Oh, Agatha," Jane said wearily, "I know exactly what you thought. You thought to promote a match between us, but even you must see how unsuitable such a match would be. Miss Propriety and the Rake! No, no! It is too absurd to be thought of."

At the last, Jane had managed to inject a note of amusement into her voice. But as she was unable to look at her companion as she spoke, she did not see the sudden look of determination which crossed Agatha's face.

That expression, however, had vanished when Jane turned towards her once more. "Speaking of matches, Agatha, just what is going on between you and Sir Alfred?"

Astonishingly, Agatha blushed before saying, "I cannot imagine what you mean, Jane. It is true that we have been spending a great deal of time together, but that is only because the Manor has been so understaffed. Then, too, there is Sir Alfred's gout. It is improving steadily, but it would not be doing so if he were left to himself. The man needs a keeper."

"Indeed," said Jane.

"Yes," continued Agatha, busily smoothing an invisible wrinkle from her skirt, "so I have been attempting to keep him in line. Also, although several of his staff have returned, his housekeeper is unable to do so just yet. As a result, Sir Alfred and I thought this would be an excellent opportunity to instruct Alice in the management of a household."

"Oh, Agatha," Jane said, "you should not be burdened with that chore. But never mind, I shall be able to take Alice off your hands now."

"Oh, no!" cried Agatha. Then, blushing again, she said, "To be perfectly truthful, my dear, I rather enjoy playing the role of teacher again, and I have discovered that Alice learns quite rapidly. Also, I have more or less promised Sir Alfred that she and I will come each day until his housekeeper can return. So, if you do not mind, I should like to continue with this portion of Alice's instruction."

Jane longed to say that she minded very much, but of course she could not. Instead she said, "Well, only if you are certain that *you* do not mind."

"Not in the least," Agatha assured her cheerfully. Then she added, "And since I have another full day ahead of me tomorrow, I believe I, too, shall retire."

Standing, she patted Jane's cheek. "Good night, my dear," she said softly. "Do not stay up too late."

"No, I shan't," murmured Jane.

Then she sat, staring at the door through which Agatha had departed, wondering what she was going to do now. She had counted upon having Alice to help occupy her time, but that would not be possible. At least, not for the immediate future, and it was that which she feared the most. She knew in her head, if not in her heart, that time would eventually ease her pain, but in the meantime, she needed something to keep her occupied.

Of course there were always her usual household chores. They had certainly kept her busy enough in the past, but not in the way she now needed. Because they were so routine, she knew that her mind would be free to wander, and that would not do. No, she must think of something else.

It was several minutes before the very thing came to her. Her tenants! She would spend tomorrow visiting each one of them. She would listen to their gossip and their troubles and give them the benefit of her advice. Surely one or two would be in need of her medical services. And, while she was about it, it might be a good notion to invite Mr. Davies to accompany her. It would be an excellent opportunity for him to meet her people.

Oh, yes. That should fill her day quite nicely. And after tomorrow, she was certain that Mr. Davies would appreciate her help and advice until he grew more accustomed to his new responsibilities. That should see her through the remainder of the week, by which time, she hoped, Sir Alfred's housekeeper would have returned.

Unfortunately, Jane's plans went awry.

It all began well enough. Mr. Davies gladly accepted her invitation to visit her tenants with her; it was a beautiful day; and she was driving her curricle, which was one of her favourite things to do. But almost from the moment they stepped into the first cottage, nothing went as she had visualized.

All of her people seemed to be enjoying the most extraordinary degree of good health. Of course she was extremely glad of that, but there was not so much as a child's scraped knee to require her attention. Even worse, no one wished to speak of anything or anyone but St. Clair, for whom they had nothing but praise.

And then there was poor Mr. Davies. Not by word or deed did he reveal his disappointment, but Jane soon realized that he was far from comfortable. Only then did it strike her that these visits were not what he had expected or wished for. It was the men whom he needed to meet and talk with, and they were all out, working in the fields.

And so, after a very short stop at each cottage, Jane dutifully drove her estate agent out to the fields, where he happily spent what seemed an inordinate amount of time talking with each male tenant. All of which meant that, with so much time on her hands, she spent the entire day doing just what she was trying to avoid—thinking of St. Clair.

Nor did anything else fall in with her schedule for the remainder of the week.

Although Mr. Davies was unfailingly polite and deferential when Jane sought him out early the next morning, she quickly sensed his impatience and frustration. It was quite apparent that he had no need of her help or her advice, for he knew his business very well. So that scheme was abandoned almost before it was begun.

But with the long hours of the entire sennight stretching out before her, she was filled with both dismay and panic. How on earth was she going to fill all of them?

Then a happy thought occurred to her. Madame Estelle had not yet delivered the gowns she had ordered, and Jane decided that she would drive into Leeds and collect them herself. While she was there, she would call at the infirmary to see how the young urchin was faring.

In fact, she decided, if he was up to making the journey, she would bring him back to Meadowbrook with her. The fresh country air and good food would do wonders for him, and she was certain that she and Mr. Davies could find something useful for him to do on the estate.

Her first errand was successful. The gowns were completed, but Madame Estelle had not yet had time to arrange for their delivery, and so Jane was able to take them with her. It was a small thing, but after her failures of the past two days, it seemed a good omen. She arrived at the infirmary feeling almost light-hearted.

That made her disappointment all the keener when she learned that the child was no longer there. Nor could she discover what had become of him, for the busy matron could tell her only that the boy had been claimed and taken away that very morning by a most rough-looking individual.

Jane had no doubt that the individual had been the chimney-sweep. Even if she could discover their whereabouts, there was no way she could wrest the boy from the man's clutches. No matter how cruel and in-humane he might be, the law was on his side. So that now, in addition to all her other troubles, she was consumed by guilt over that pitiful child's fate, for she knew that if she had come a day sooner, she might have saved him.

To make matters worse, if that were possible, the trip to Leeds had served to remind her more strongly than ever of St. Clair. For most of the return trip she was sunk in self-pity and despair.

By the time Jane reached Meadowbrook, however, she had regained a great deal of her common sense and concluded that she had wasted far too much time in these fruitless efforts to stay busy. She would do much better to resume her usual daily routine. Having discovered that it was impossible to suppress thoughts and memories of St. Clair, she decided that she would no longer make the attempt, but might just as well give them full rein. To do so was painful, but it was a bittersweet pain, and almost comforting in an odd sort of way.

As it happened, things were not so bad as she had thought they would be. She was kept far busier than she had expected, for Elsie played least in sight even more often than was usual. But for once Jane did not really mind and scarcely listened to the girl's vague excuses the first few times Jane questioned her.

Although a certain heaviness in her chest never quite left her, Jane discovered that even so profound an emotion as grief could not afflict one continuously. There were times, however rare, when she actually forgot her troubles…or at least did not think of them overmuch.

Then, too, Agatha and Alice were there every evening, for they did not again dine at the Manor with the squire. It was from Agatha Jane learned the reason for Elsie's frequent defections.

"Well, dear," said Agatha, "she has been seeing one of the footmen at Ethridge Hall. In fact, I should not be surprised if she gave you her notice very soon now."

"Well," Jane said wryly, "I cannot say that it would be a great loss. And now that we have Mr. Davies, we should be able to hire someone more competent."

"Yes," agreed Agatha.

Before Jane could wonder too much at the lack of conviction in Agatha's voice, Alice said, "I am surprised you did not know about Elsie and her footman. It is common knowledge in the neighbourhood." Then, with a sly glance at Agatha, she added, "It seems that there is a great deal of romance in the air of late."

For everyone but me, mused Jane as she studied Agatha thoughtfully. For some time, the suspicion had been growing in her mind that Agatha might be developing a *tendre* for Sir Alfred. But, despite her words to St. Clair, she had been able to dismiss such a possibility as being too fantastical. Now she was not so certain, especially as she watched a fiery blush spread over Agatha's cheeks. Nevertheless, she had no intention of discussing the matter in Alice's presence, and so she changed the subject.

However, as soon as she and her companion were alone later that evening, she demanded, "Now, Agatha, just what is going on between you and Sir Alfred?"

"Well, dear, I have been meaning to tell you, only I wished to wait until...well, no matter. The truth is that I have come to care for Alfred a great deal."

"Oh, Agatha, I don't wish to cast a damper on your happiness, but do you think that is wise?" Then, before Agatha could reply, Jane continued, "But what a stupid question! I doubt that any female is wise when it comes to men. It is just that I do not wish to see you hurt."

"Well, you can put your mind at ease on that score, for I shan't be hurt," Agatha told her. "You see, now that he has recovered from his gout, Alfred means to go to the Continent after all, and he has asked me to go with him."

At Jane's expression, Agatha laughed and said, "Oh, do not look so shocked, love. It is not a carte blanche he has offered me, but marriage. And I have accepted, so it will be our wedding trip, although we shall take Alice with us."

For a moment, Jane did not know what to say. All she could do was wonder how she would survive now that she was losing Agatha, too. But then, shamed at such selfishness, she managed to smile and say, "Then I must wish you happy. And I *do* wish you happiness, for no one deserves it more. But there is no need to take Alice with you on your wedding trip. She can remain here with me."

"No, no," said Agatha, her eyes twinkling merrily, "she will be no trouble for us. But I do not plan to desert you just yet. Alfred and I have agreed to postpone the wedding and the trip until your affairs are settled."

Jane did not attempt to discourage Agatha, for she knew that she could not live here alone without a companion to lend her countenance. That was not what held her silent, however. She was considering a most daring plan for settling her own affairs, and wondering if she had the courage to see it through.

AT THAT VERY MOMENT, St. Clair was demanding of Kearny, "What the devil do you mean by saying that she is going to marry that old reprobate? Damnation! I *told* her not to encourage him!"

Kearny gave an elaborate shrug and said, "All's I know is what I heard when I stopped over at the Hall after getting the boy. One o' your footmen had it straight from the lady's own maid. 'A certain spinster what lives at Meadowbrook,' he says to me, 'is about to be leg-shackled to the old squire.'"

"Indeed!" said St. Clair with narrowed eyes. Then he added as he strode towards the door, "We shall see about that!"

CHAPTER SEVENTEEN

TWO MORNINGS later, Jane sat at her writing table surrounded by wads of discarded paper and chewed on the end of her pen as she gazed down at yet another blank sheet. It had taken her a long time to build up her courage, and now she was finding it amazingly difficult to find the right words. How *did* one go about offering to become a man's mistress?

With a deep sigh, she dipped the dry pen in the inkwell and began again.

My Dear St. Clair,
    Since our last conversation, I have reached the conclusion that you were wrong. After giving the matter a great deal of thought, I have decided that I am, after all, perfectly willing to settle for less than marriage.

Jane paused and was trying to decide what next to say when she was distracted by a thunderous pounding. It sounded, in fact, as if someone were using a battering ram on the front doors. The noise then ceased abruptly.

Rising from her chair, she hurried over to place her ear against her chamber door. Unfortunately, she could hear nothing beyond a murmuring of voices.

Hoping to hear more, she eased her door open, although by now an irrational premonition had her heart pounding so loudly that she doubted it would help.

Nevertheless, Melrose's voice came to her quite clearly. "But, sir, indeed, you cannot—"

He was interrupted by another voice, unmistakably St. Clair's, shouting, "Jane! Get down here immediately! You have exactly five minutes to present yourself, or I shall come up there!"

She did not doubt him for a second, and as she splashed her face with cold water and ran a brush hurriedly through her hair, she vacillated between extremes of hope and fear. Why was he here? Had he discovered that he missed her as much as she missed him? She could not help but ask herself why he should have come unless he *did* care for her, yet she feared being hurt again if she were wrong.

She winced as she took a final glance in the mirror. She was wearing one of her oldest gowns and she looked as if she had been thrown together all by guess. But at least she was presentable enough to show herself, and in time to prevent St. Clair from charging up the stairs and into her chamber. Still, as she made her way down the stairs, she found that her knees were shaking and her hands trembling. She could not remember ever having been so nervous in all her life.

Melrose nodded toward the drawing-room and muttered, "He's in there, Miss Jane."

"Thank you, Melrose," she said.

Then, taking a deep breath, and with her head held high, she entered the drawing-room, intending to ask him what he meant by disturbing her household in such an outrageous way. But at the sight of him, she was rendered speechless.

He was attired in rumpled evening clothes; his hair looked as though it had not seen a comb or brush in a sennight, and his eyes were slightly bloodshot with dark circles under them. He must have been imbibing heavily, or else he had travelled straight through from London without sleep. Since she could detect no telltale odour of strong spirits, Jane had to surmise that the latter was the case. And despite herself, hope rose more strongly in her breast.

His eyes raked over her, and to her surprise, since he was scowling quite ferociously, he remarked, "I have never seen your hair down like that. I like it."

"Th-thank you," she said, just barely stopping herself from reaching up to touch her hair like some coy schoolgirl. "But, St. Clair, what are you doing here?"

"Ha!" he said, glaring even more fiercely. "I came to prevent a *certain spinster* from going through with her plan to marry Sir Alfred. That is what I am doing here." Then, running his fingers through his already dishevelled hair, he exclaimed, "Good God, Jane, the man is an over-aged loose screw. I could scarcely believe the news when I heard it. In fact, I would not have believed it had I not had it from Kearny, who swore that it came directly from your own maid."

Jane frowned, thinking it odd that he should be so overset by Agatha's marriage plans, but she only asked, "How did Kearny learn of it?"

"He stopped at Ethridge Hall for a few days after he retrieved our young urchin from the infirmary in Leeds."

Jane gasped. "Then Kearny was the rough-looking man who took him. Oh, Jon, thank you for rescuing him. But I wish you had told me what you meant to do. You cannot know how I have worried about that child."

"Yes, well, I am sorry for that, but you might have guessed that I could not leave him there. He would have ended in a foundling home or the workhouse, or worse."

"Yes, that is what I was afraid of."

"However," he said, frowning again, "you are attempting to change the subject, and I have not finished what I came to say."

"Very well," she replied, "but could we not sit down and be more comfortable while you say it?"

"Certainly," he answered, and graciously offered her a seat on her own sofa.

When she was settled, he sat opposite her, and leaned forward with his elbows on his knees. "I think I understand why you came to this decision, Jane. But really, my dear, it will not do. Good God! The man is old enough to be your father, and even worse, he is a member of the Prince Regent's set, which is no recommendation at all!"

Jane stared at him blankly for a moment, but as the full realization of his misconception dawned upon her, she could not resist teasing him. She sighed and said, "Oh, St. Clair, I scarcely know how to tell you this, but I fear you have come on a sleeveless errand. You see, I agree with you completely."

St. Clair straightened as though he had been slapped, scowled again, and demanded, "What the devil?"

"Yes," Jane told him with another heavy sigh. "I had already decided that such a marriage would not do, although I believe that Sir Alfred means to change his ways."

"Well, I am certainly glad that you came to your senses in time," he said. "But whatever possessed you even to consider such a thing?"

He looked so peeved that she could no longer hold back her laughter. Finally she said, "Oh, St. Clair, I am sorry but, truly, I could not resist quizzing you."

"Yes, you are having a great deal of fun at my expense, are you not? But perhaps it is time to let me in on the joke."

"It was too bad of me, I know, but you really should have guessed the truth. It is Agatha who plans to marry Sir Alfred, not I."

"Agatha!" he exclaimed. Then he said rather sheepishly, "Well, it seems I am guilty of jumping to false conclusions." He paused before adding, "But if Agatha is to be married, you will be in the market for

a new companion, will you not? Do you have someone in mind?''

Realizing that she would never have a better opportunity to make her offer, Jane swallowed and said,
"Actually I do, though not the sort you are likely to
be imagining. I was thinking more along the lines of
a...a male companion.''

"What nonsense are you talking now?" he growled.

Jane felt as if her cheeks must be on fire, but did her
best to ignore the sensation as she forced herself to say,
"Well, St. Clair, I have learned, since last seeing you,
that I am a great deal more like my mother than I ever
knew.'' She paused to gather courage. "The truth is
that I have discovered in myself a most reprehensible
fondness for rakes.''

One of his eyebrows rose very slowly before he
asked suspiciously, "Are you, by any chance, hinting
for an offer from me?"

Jane searched his eyes, and finding a trace of the
familiar laughter there, took even more courage.
Enough courage to say, "Well, yes, but you needn't
worry. I am well aware that you are not in the market
for a wife. Of course I should prefer you as a husband, but...''

She could not go on. It was almost more than she
could do, to continue gazing at him unflinchingly
when what she really felt like doing was hiding her face
in her hands. She could not believe that *she,* of all
people, had spoken so brazenly.

To make matters worse, his eyes now held an un-holy gleam as he drawled, "Just what is it you are trying to say, Jane?"

Her heart sank as she realized that she was going to be obliged to put her proposition into words. But she could not back down now. Raising her chin bravely she said, "I am offering to become your mistress."

"I see," he said. "And just what put this notion into your head?"

"Well, to be perfectly frank, it was Agatha."

"Agatha!" he exclaimed. "What the devil was she about to make such a suggestion?"

"No, no! She would never suggest such a thing. It was something she said which gave me the idea. I first thought of it when she mentioned something about a *carte blanche,* and since I had learned from Elsie that Lady Cathcart had not gone with you to London, I thought..."

He was not helping her a bit, but merely watching her with an interested expression on his face, so she said defiantly, "Well, you *did* kiss me on more than one occasion, so I thought perhaps you would not find such an alliance too distasteful, and—for God's sake, St. Clair, will you please say something and stop me from babbling like this?"

Although she thought one corner of his mouth twitched slightly, he continued to study her closely, and it seemed like forever before he said, "I think, my dear, that you would do better to marry me, rather than fall victim to another rake or even a highway-man. There is no telling what fate might befall you if left to your own devices. No, I really cannot allow you to go about offering yourself in this way."

"No, no, St. Clair," she said with a small laugh. "You cannot think that I would go through this again. Good God! It was difficult enough with you. But, my dear friend, I care for you too much to allow you to sacrifice yourself in a loveless marriage. In fact..." She stopped because he had risen as she spoke.

Drawing her to her feet, too, he said, "If you do not know by now, my girl, that I am head over ears in love with you, then you are even greener than I thought."

And, to punctuate his words, he wrapped his arms around her and kissed her in such a way as to banish all her doubts. In truth, he was so passionate that his former kisses seemed quite tame, and by the time it was over, Jane was breathless.

But at last he drew back slightly and said, "Well, my love?"

"Well?" she repeated dazedly.

"Are you not going to tell me that you love me, too?"

"Oh! But Jon," she said, "you must know that I do. I have loved you since you were a highwayman."

He laughed and hugged her close again, saying, "Oh, Jane, thank God for your sharpshooting coachman."

She was enjoying that hug a great deal when he pulled away and said with a slight frown, "However, since you are so very fond of rakes, I fear you will be disappointed in me. You see, I have grown tired of my wild ways and have already begun repairing my reputation. In fact, my love, you are liable to find me too tame by half.''

But Jane only smiled and shook her head, then drew his mouth back down to hers. For she knew that, though he might no longer be a rake, to her, he would always be her own beloved highwayman.

HARLEQUIN®

REGENCY ◆ ROMANCE™

Deck the halls . . .

You'll be dreaming of mistletoe right along with our
Regency heroines this holiday season when you meet the
men of *their* dreams.

Celebrate the holidays with some of your favourite authors
as they regale you with heartwarming stories of
Christmas past.

In November, get in the spirit with *Mistletoe and Mischief*
by Patricia Wynn. In December, curl up with
Sarah's Angel by Judith Stafford and *A Christmas Bride* by
Brenda Hiatt. Then enjoy.

Harlequin Regency Romance—our gift to you.

Available wherever Harlequin books are sold.

1993 Keepsake

Stories

Capture the spirit and romance of Christmas with KEEPSAKE CHRISTMAS STORIES, a collection of three stories by favorite historical authors. The perfect Christmas gift!

Don't miss these heartwarming stories, available in November wherever Harlequin books are sold:

ONCE UPON A CHRISTMAS by Curtiss Ann Matlock
A FAIRYTALE SEASON by Marianne Willman
TIDINGS OF JOY by Victoria Pade

ADD A TOUCH OF ROMANCE TO YOUR HOLIDAY SEASON WITH KEEPSAKE CHRISTMAS STORIES!

HX93

**FLASH:
ROMANCE
MAKES
HISTORY!**

History the Harlequin way, that is. Our books invite you to experience a past you never read about in grammar school!

Travel back in time with us, and pirates will sweep you off your feet, cowboys will capture your heart, and noblemen will lead you to intrigue and romance, *always* romance—because that's what makes each Harlequin Historical title a thrilling escape for you, four times every month. Just think of the adventures you'll have!

So pick up a Harlequin Historical novel today, and relive history in your wildest dreams....

**Fifty red-blooded, white-hot, true-blue hunks
from every State in the Union!**

Look for MEN MADE IN AMERICA! Written by some of our most poplar authors, these stories feature fifty of the strongest, sexiest men, each from a different state in the union!

Two titles available every other month at your favorite retail outlet.

In November, look for:

STRAIGHT FROM THE HEART by Barbara Delinsky (Connecticut)
AUTHOR'S CHOICE by Elizabeth August (Delaware)

In January, look for:

DREAM COME TRUE by Ann Major (Florida)
WAY OF THE WILLOW by Linda Shaw (Georgia)

You won't be able to resist MEN MADE IN AMERICA!

When the only time you have for yourself is...

STOLEN *moments* ™

Christmas is such a busy time—with shopping, decorating, writing
cards, trimming trees, wrapping gifts....

When you do have a few *stolen moments* to call your own, treat yourself
to a brand-new *short* novel. Relax with one of our Stocking Stuffers—
or with all six!

Each STOLEN MOMENTS title
is a complete and original contemporary romance that's the perfect
length for the busy woman of the nineties! Especially at Christmas...

And they make perfect **stocking stuffers,** too! (For your mother,
grandmother, daughters, friends, co-workers, neighbors, aunts,
cousins—all the other women in your life!)

Look for the STOLEN MOMENTS display in December

STOCKING STUFFERS:

HIS MISTRESS Carrie Alexander
DANIEL'S DECEPTION Marie DeWitt
SNOW ANGEL Isolde Evans
THE FAMILY MAN Danielle Kelly
THE LONE WOLF Ellen Rogers
MONTANA CHRISTMAS Lynn Russell

HSM2

 WORLDWIDE LIBRARY ®

Relive the romance...
Harlequin and Silhouette
are proud to present

by Request™

A program of collections of three complete novels by the most-requested
authors with the most-requested themes. Be sure to look for one volume each
month with three complete novels by top-name authors.

In September: **BAD BOYS**   Dixie Browning
                                                         Ann Major
                                                         Ginna Gray
No heart is safe when these hot-blooded hunks are in town!

In October: **DREAMSCAPE**   Jayne Ann Krentz
                                                         Anne Stuart
                                                       Bobby Hutchinson
Something's happening! But is it love or magic?

In December: **SOLUTION: MARRIAGE** Debbie Macomber
                                                         Annette Broadrick
                                                       Heather Graham Pozzessere
Marriages in name only have a way of leading to love....

Available at your favorite retail outlet.

REQ-G2

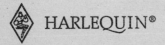 HARLEQUIN®   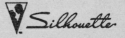 *Silhouette*